(YEAH, I DIDN'T BELIEVE IT EITHER.)

Paridise Kau

For Kylie, Shari, and Duke.
Thank you for giving me the courage to follow
my dreams.
I love you guys!

Note

So, I want to start by saying that you are a complete *asshole* for not telling me about this assignment until the end of my <u>JUNIOR</u> <u>YEAR!!</u>

And that you're making me write this with pen and paper!? Like seriously, do you want to kill me? This is going to take up so much of my summer break, you <u>sadist.</u>

And I know that what I'm about to do is petty and way more work in the long run, but since you're making me do this and not giving me an option too, like, I don't know, do a presentation or something, I'm going to make this horrible for you too.

This is my revenge.

Hope you enjoy it!

:)

♣ Chapter 1 ♣

I decided to separate this into chapters because it will be easier for me to finish if I have an outline for everything. Did I mention that you wanted <u>everything</u> we did in our four years of High School? (Happy grading, you fool.) And just to make this even sweeter, I'm gonna start from the very beginning!

You brought this on yourself; remember that.

Okay, here we go:

A long time ago, the first person on record who had gotten superpowers was born in Venice, Italy. They could move water with their mind (Which, what a city to have that power in, my god.). At first, they tried to use their powers for good. But, eventually, they moved to the dark side, causing worldwide chaos and panic. And then people who had developed abilities (or had them the whole time) decided to come together to fight against the world's first-ever 'superhero.' They dubbed themselves Vigilantes of justice (Cliche name, I know), and–

I'm kidding.

I'm not going THAT far back.

Made you sweat, didn't I?

I'm actually going to start from when I got the acceptance letter:

It was like every other day before the summer break. I.e., Nobody, not even the teachers, wanted to do any work. So, we all decided to watch the fight that flooded the news stations instead. I didn't mind; I always liked that kind of stuff, so getting to watch it before I got home was a bonus. I didn't have to share the TV with my little sister, who would always just push me out of the way before I could even put in a single word of protest.

. . .I can feel you judging me, and it's not even the fourth paragraph. Also, who are you to judge? You know, considering, well, everything you've ever done? *Whatever.* My sister can be scarier than any superhero when you get in the way of her limited TV time. She can be a devil in a nine-year-old's body. Nobody wants to deal with that literal tornado.

Bite me.

The teacher had just turned on the classroom projector when my best friend leaned in close, his hand shielding his mouth, "So, who do you want to win?"

It was a rhetorical question, of course. I mean, only insane people would root for the 'superhero.' (Like, Duh?) I told him as much with a roll of my eyes, "Obviously, I want the vigilante to win. Why are you *like this?*"

He shrugged, but I could tell by the smirk on his face that he does it just to annoy me. And honestly, he can get away with it pretty easily. We've known each other for so long that it would have been weird if he didn't try anything. Like, are-you-okay-should-I-call-an-ambulance kind of weird.

I met Alex when my mom brought me over to his house for a 'playdate,' and we quickly argued over who our favorite vigilante was (*cough* Nightshade *cough*). We hated each other for a long time before we both decided that it was too much effort to keep the argument going, so, boom! Our friendship officially formed. Also, it helped that his mom's made the best cookies in the universe. All chocolate chippy goodness. . .my mouth's watering just thinking about it.

Alex leaned back into his chair as my teacher turned up the volume. We watched with rapt attention as the showdown between the vigilante CleanSweep and the superhero Gravity Mask went full swing. I'm not going to write out what happened; watch the recording like everybody else. Last I checked, the video had at least 30 million views, so who knows, maybe you have already seen it by now? (Not that I care, really. Do what you want.)

It's always fun to rewatch the more badass videos. It takes me back to a simpler time. A time before, I had to think about what was *really* going on in them. Well, Triston was more to blame, but I'm mad at *you*, so it's all *your* fault. So, thanks for ruining my childhood.

Anyway, everyone in the class cheered as CleanSweep won the battle with a powerful attack straight to Gravity Masks' face. He punched him right in the jaw. Knockout! (Guess you don't need to look it up. You're welcome.)

Alex turned to me, his face overflowing with amazement and awe, you know, his usual fanboy expression, "Did you see that! That was *awesome!* He hit him like *wham* but first took him down like *swoosh!*"

I swear I couldn't help it. Really. But I didn't regret saying, "You could say he *swept* the floor with him."

Alex only paused to tell me that was the lamest thing he had ever heard before he continued to passionately explain the battle with sound effects. The bell rang in the middle of an Alex-made *'thwack!'* and everyone paused before rushing out of the classroom and into the hallway.

I grabbed my bag from the side of my desk and hoisted it on my shoulder, Alex following my lead. Shuffling into the hallway (after saying bye to Mrs. Parks), I weaved through students, who all had an air of excitement that wasn't just the invigorating feeling of escaping educational jail. The halls were filled with gossip, mainly about the fight everyone just watched, and the excitement followed us to the sidewalk lined with school buses.

Goodbye, middle school. It was nice knowing ya!

We crossed the street and started our trek back home. Living only four blocks away from school had its perks but, still, I was regretting my decision not to ride my bike because the air was unbelievably hot. Heck, I would have taken my old junky roller skates out of my closet if it got me out of the heat faster. My bag felt heavy on my shoulders, and I wondered to myself why I procrastinated cleaning out my locker until now, on the last day of school, like an idiot. I envied Alex's almost completely deflated bag. I was pretty sure he didn't even have anything in there worth toting the bag around anyway! So why did he even bring it?

(I just realized I'm rambling, and I'm writing this on paper. God, this is so dumb.)

We arrived at our houses, sweaty and ready to get inside to the sweet mercy of the aircon, but not even thirty seconds after we got home, my little sister, Jamie, slammed open the front door so hard I swore that the house shook, "Sky! There's some weird guy here to see you!"

You=weird guy. Still cracks me up. Hahaha.

My thoughts came out lamely through my lips, "Huh?"

Jamie rolled her dark brown eyes, stomped down our walkway with all the confidence of a nine-year-old on a mission, and grabbed my wrist, "God, why are you so dumb? Hurry up!"

"Okay, okay! Let go!" I yanked my arm out of her grip and followed her into the house. I made sure to glance back at Alex, who looked a mixture of concerned and amused. His expression was mostly amused now that I think about it, that traitor, "See you later."

Alex saluted me, "Good luck?"

"Thanks!" I yelled sarcastically from my front porch.

"Anytime!" Alex shouted back before hopping up the stairs, swinging open his door, and closing it with a soft slam. I huffed in only slight annoyance before Jamie got a hold of my wrist again and hauled me through the front door, almost tripping me in the process. She dragged me through the main hallway and into the kitchen before she let go. I rubbed my wrist and glared at her, but she just gave me an unimpressed look and pointed towards the dining table, where a stranger sat with my parents.

I'm trying to decide how I should describe you, seeing as this might get me extra credit points if I do this right. But then again, that ship kind of sailed when I called you an asshole (and weird), so why should I hold back now?

You were sitting at our table with an expression I should have known was too easy-going to be authentic and making small talk with my mother, who was buying your act hook, line, and sinker. You even had the sense to dress professionally in a suit and tie with your black hair styled in a way that said, 'Hey, I'm not a total weirdo' and 'I'm totally a responsible adult, you can trust me with your child! *wink*'.

It was my dad who noticed me first, "Skylar, you're home. There's someone who's here to see you."

"I can see that," I said as I plopped my bag on the kitchen counter, vaguely noticing when Jamie leaned against it behind me, "Should I be worried?"

My dad raised an eyebrow, "Should you? Is there something you need to tell me?"

"Uh," I said before deflecting quickly and sticking out my hand for you to shake, "Skylar. Nice to meet you!"

Dad gave me a look that was all eyebrows but shook his head as he let my suspicious behavior slide. Maybe it was because of the news you were about to share, or perhaps he just didn't want to deal with it while you were in the room? Either way, you took my hand in a firm shake.

At least you don't shake hands like your arm is a soggy noodle.

I can respect *that*, at least.

I waited for you to say your name before realizing that you weren't going to and dropped my hand, "Uh, okay then."

"Sky, don't be rude," My mother reprimanded. I remember that I wanted to blurt out that it was rude not to say your name in an introduction, but I decided against it. Unaware of my thoughts, Mom's face morphed to look more excited, "This man is here to tell you about a great opportunity!"

That's when I started to get the feeling that this was too...sudden? Planned? Weird? Infomercial-like? I felt uneasy. For all I knew, they could have been sending me to military school or something (Do people even do that anymore?). I mean, I don't think I did anything to make them do that. But still, her statement could go both ways, and I wasn't sure if this was good or bad.

Wary is the right word.

I was wary.

I stood there awkwardly as you reached into your coat pocket and pulled out a letter, the back of the envelope stamped shut with a wax seal. My first thought was if people still used wax seals on their letters, but your following sentence quickly drew my attention away from the wax, "Mr. Hayes, please open this."

Everyone's eyes were on me as I tore through the envelope, and the silence was way too loud. My face wrinkled as I pulled out the crisp white paper inside, unfolded it, and read the words that I was surprised to see where written out in neat handwriting:

To Mr. Skylar Hayes,

  We are happy to inform you that you have been selected by lottery to partake in our new program at Freedom Bay Highschool. If you accept our offer, you will be enrolled immediately in our school under a scholarship. We will also take care of any expenses you may require in the four years you'll attend our school. We pride ourselves on giving youths many skills for the future and have almost a 100% success rate. If you have any questions about enrollment or anything else, please ask our representative.

  We look forward to your decision and hope to hear from you soon.

  Best wishes,

  The Principal of Freedom Bay Highschool,

  Triston McCully

  (Did I just copy down the letter word for word? Yes, yes I did.)

  I stared at the paper far longer than I probably should have before I asked, "Freedom Bay? Where the heck is that? I don't think I've ever heard of this school."

Before my parents could look scandalized, you leaned forward in your chair, "Freedom Bay High School is located just off the coast of Hawaii, on a private island."

The letter slipped through my fingers and silently drifted to the floor, "On a what!?"

My mom leaned forward, a giant smile on her face, but her eyes told me to behave at the same time. It's probably a mom thing, "It's also rated the top high school in the country. It's tough to get into, and they're offering to let you go for free! Isn't that exciting, Sky!"

"Wait, wait, wait! So Skylar gets to go to a school on an *island?* That's *so* not fair." Jamie ranted behind me. I forgot that she was still in the kitchen. Heck, I kind of forgot about a lot of things because my brain was still stuck on the private island part!

"Jamie! Don't be disrespectful." My father chided through my swirling thoughts.

Jamie crossed her arms with a huff, stomped out of the kitchen and into the living room.

Dad smiled apologetically, "Sorry about that. She's in her rebellious phase."

"Don't worry about it. I'm a teacher, so I completely understand," You said with a charming smile before turning to me. I was still frozen, but your words helped me out of it, "Mr. Hayes, Skylar, what do you say? Do you want to come to our school?"

I wasn't sure what to say at first. I was honestly leaning towards not going at all. I didn't want to go to some preppy school away from my friends and family, even if it was on a private island. In Hawaii. But I also couldn't just say no either. My mother looked so happy to hear the news, and my dad was equally so. Would I disappoint them if I didn't go?

You sighed and looked at your clasped hands on the table, "I see. This is a hard decision to make. You probably don't want to leave your family and friends. I get that. I wouldn't want to either. So how about this, Skylar?"

You stood up and leaned against the table, relaxed, "What would you say if I told you we could fly you back home every month? We do this for all our attendees if they want to, so it wouldn't be a problem. And if you're thinking something along the lines of 'this is too preppy of a school for me,' I can guarantee you that this school will surprise you. Sure, there will probably be a class you hate, but if you go, you will gain something. . .much more *life-changing* than just a standard high school degree."

You paused for only a moment, thinking through your words carefully, "The principal will understand if you say no. There is no pressure and no obligation to attend, but I think you would fit in well at our school. I know that this will probably sound cheesy, but you can do great things if you put your mind to it."

During your speech, your eyes slowly moved up to look into mine. Then you extended your hand, "What do you say, Skylar?"

I'll have to begrudgingly admit that at that moment, you were at least kind of cool. Don't let it get to your head, though.

I swallowed, nervous, "Can I think about it?"

You dropped your arm but didn't seem offended, "Sure. I'll leave my contact info. If you have any questions, give me a call."

"No, uh, can I just have a minute? You don't have to leave. I just. . .need to step outside for a second." I said.

You tilted your head in slight confusion but played along anyway, ". . .Alright."

I nodded before backing out of the room. My parents looked at each other and then back at me, then back at each other, but I was already in the hallway before they could say anything. Once I was out of sight, I ran to the front door, opened it, and sprinted across the street. I banged on Alex's door hard and loud, "Alex! C'mon man, open the door!"

"It's already open!" I heard Alex shout before he appeared in the doorway, his expression worried but also curious, "What's going on?"

I moved to show Alex the letter before realizing that it was still on the floor in my dining room. I dropped my hand and stood there stiffly for a moment. Alex was uncharacteristically patient as he leaned against his open doorway and waited for me to speak.

I cleared my throat, "Uh... so you know how someone was waiting to see me, right?"

"...Yeah?" Alex prompted.

"Well, he was some teacher from a famous high school that wants to recruit me, and I don't know what to do because it's on a private island, and I can fly home and call you anytime. But I won't be able to go to the same high school, and what if it's too preppy? But he said that it wouldn't be, but can I trust the guy?"

Alex blinked at me as he took in the words, then, "Did you just say private island?"

Everyone loves to get stuck on the private island part, huh?

"Yeah," I sighed as I realized that I had been just spouting hypersonic word vomit, "But that's not why I came over here."

Alex pushed himself off the doorframe and straightened up, "You came over here to ask if I minded, right?"

"I guess?"

"Well, do you want to go?" Alex asked curiously.

"I don't. . .know?"

"Alright, let's try this again. Would you regret it if you didn't?"

Ouch. Thinking back, I realize now how mature Alex was at that moment. We only just finished eighth grade! We were going to graduate that weekend. And here he was helping me make serious life decisions, "Probably? I mean, this is supposed to be the best school in the country so. . ."

"Well, if you came over to hear my opinion, of course I don't want you to go," I opened my mouth, but he shushed me, ". . .because I'm selfish, and I'll miss you. But if you feel like this would be for the best, I'll support you. What kind of friend would I be if I didn't?"

Alex smiled as he raised his clenched fist for a fist bump, "Plus, you could always just drop out and come back, right? I mean, I wouldn't be surprised. I don't understand why they would want you anyway."

I swatted his hand away, "Gee, thanks."

Alex laughed but raised his fist and waited. I glared at him, but there wasn't much heat to it, so eventually, I caved and fist-bumped him back, "I guess I could try it out. And I could always change my mind before I have to go. . ."

"Exactly. And who knows. . ." Alex grinned, ". . .maybe you'll somehow become a vigilante while you're gone. Fall into a vat of radioactive waste or something, Ooo-wee-oooh!"

"Oh, shut up," I scoffed, and Alex burst out laughing.

Okay, I know, I know, that was the universe trying to foreshadow my life, wasn't it? But can you blame me for not seeing it at the time? How was I supposed to know that the school I would be attending was a school for vigilantes? Like, who in their right mind would think that was a thing?

And yet, despite the universe's warning, I went back to my house, accepted your offer, and sealed my fate.

And I don't regret it.

Not one bit.

♣ Chapter 2 ♣

Before I knew it, summer break was over, but that didn't stop Alex and me from trying to squeeze in as much fun as possible before we had to go our separate ways.

On Alex's birthday (June 24th), we went to an amusement park and rode every rollercoaster until we were sick. On July 4th, we went swimming at the lake, and Alex sent my sister flying from her inner tube (her poor popsicle was never recovered). On one eventful night in August, we gushed over a Vigilante saving a town near to ours and couldn't stop talking about it for days. I stuffed myself full of Bethany's cookies, and she promised she'd make more when I would visit. . .

It was probably the best summer vacation I ever had.

But slowly, the days passed, and then it was time for me to go.

It was bittersweet when I had to catch my flight to Hawaii on the last day of the break. Alex had helped me pack my suitcase, and we may or may not have gotten a little teary-eyed when I said goodbye. Yeah, I was excited, but even you would be sad to leave a friend behind. Like, sure, we could play video games online, but it wasn't the same if we couldn't try to knock the controller out of each other's hands or munch on the same bag of potato chips. . .

But I promised Alex I would keep in touch.

And I intend to keep that promise.

Always.

Anyway, that fateful morning you picked me up and drove us to the airport. We boarded a private jet (which was pretty cool at the time, not gonna lie) and flew about five hours to Hawaii in awkward silence. We were the only ones on the plane, and I remember wondering how many people were in my class and if the school had the money for a private jet for all of them.

I don't know if you remember, but I asked you about it, and you just shrugged and blew a stray hair off your face before going back to what I *have* to assume was Tinder on your phone.

I fiddled with the straps of my bag and hoped the time would fly as fast as the jet. Because

I don't know how long I would have lasted in the silence. Finally, we got off the plane a little before noon and had lunch at a homey little diner with amazing milkshakes. They were, no ARE, so good that I thought the hours of silence was worth it just to taste that shake.

Like seriously: Best. Shakes. Ever. 10/10 would recommend!!!

Then we drove to a private dock and lugged my luggage onto a boat that I would classify as a small yacht. The sun was high in the sky, and It was the first time I had ever been on anything able to float on water. So I never knew until that moment how much I *hate* boats. The swaying turned my stomach, and I tried not to gag and inevitably lose my lunch.

About maybe thirty minutes later, I looked up through my queasiness and was surprised at how big, no gigantic, the school was when we arrived. Freedom Bay Highschool has three main buildings and a central courtyard with its laughably tiny fountain (which I thought was odd at the time. I assumed that maybe the money ran out when they were building. Hmm. . .Guess I was *kinda* right?). There is also a splattering of smaller buildings with paved paths, sports-related fields/courts, and finally, what looked like a helipad on top of one of the nearby hills (helicopter included).

I stepped onto the dock feeling woozy but grateful for the steady footing. I couldn't help but stare at where I would be attending school for possibly the next four years of my life. It was like an island paradise, but it was a school, and, to be honest, it was kind of mind-blowing. I don't even know how to describe it. Maybe this is what it's like to go to college for the first time? I don't know.

I was lost in my thoughts, but I felt you put your hand on my shoulder and gently guided me off the dock and onto dry land. I was vaguely aware that someone had grabbed my bags, taking them away, and you chuckled beside me at my total awe. You didn't say anything as you steered me to the main building.

I opened the glass doors and stepped into the school's front hallway. It was so desolate that a tumbleweed could have blown by, and I wouldn't have been surprised, given how empty everything was. The lights weren't even on until we stepped further into the hall, each one flickering to life as we walked forward.

I was expecting emptiness, so I wasn't too weirded out by it. I mean, you did say that the freshman class was coming a day earlier than the rest of the students. For some sort of 'orientation exercise.' I remember that you weren't very forthcoming with information and saying, and I quote: 'Don't worry about it, we do this for all our first years. It's just a _normal orientation_, nothing _too exciting._'

Do I have to write down how much of a lie that was. . .or are you seeing the sarcasm dripping in my painstakingly handwritten italics? Maybe I should underline it a couple of times for good measure. (I decided to anyway.)

Our footsteps echoed off the lockers and down the hall until we made it to the gym. Pushing open the double doors, I was startled when fifteen pairs of eyes turned and stared right at me, all at once. I abruptly stopped in the doorway, and you ran into me from behind, which, in turn, made me stumble into the room like a total dork before straightening up and saying, ". . .Um, hi?"

I felt a little like I wanted to die when no one said anything for a couple of tense seconds. You were no help as you just walked past me like I wasn't outwardly panicking.

You raised your hand in a wave, "Sorry we're late."

My first thought was, *'Oh, god, they're still staring at me.'* until it morphed into *'Late? What do you mean late?'* as I turned to give you a questioning look. Because why would we stop for lunch if we were going to be late? You caught my eye and shrugged, leaning closer to whisper loudly, "Yeah. . .about that, we were supposed to be here *yesterday.*"

My brain shut down for all of one second before I yelled, "What!? Liar! No way that's true!"

Laughter echoed around the gym, and I realized it was coming from the only other adult, a hand covering his mouth as he gasped. That seemed to break a sliver of the tension, and everyone turned to the other man as his laughter subsided. Then, finally, he cleared his throat and smiled, "Sorry. Sorry. I shouldn't laugh. I should be scolding him!"

Mystery man gave you a stern look, but there was still a sparkle in his eyes that ruined it, "C'mon, Connor, we've talked about this. Refrain from freaking out our students on their first day, even if Skylar's face was priceless."

Before I had time to be offended, the man offered his hand out to shake, "Triston McCully. Sorry about my colleague, he means well, most of the time. I promise. Oh, and you're not late, by the way, so no need to freak out."

And that was how I met the principal of Freedom Bay Highschool, Triston McCully.

Also, I wasn't freaking out. Just internally screaming. There's a difference.

I shook his hand, and he gently grabbed my shoulder, giving it a reassuring squeeze before guiding me to the last open seat in the circle. I wasn't late, but it seemed that I was the last one to arrive. The principal took his chair in the middle and smiled, "Well then, how about we get on with this orientation? Let's start by introducing ourselves, shall we?"

I couldn't help but think this was less of an orientation and more group therapy. I mean, the chairs were arranged in a circle facing each other, and everyone looked a little uncomfortable by each other's stares. I found out that I wasn't the only one who felt the same, as the person on the left of me tapped my shoulder. I turned to see a boy with tan skin, dark hair, and blue eyes. His most defining feature was a spattering of freckles dotting his nose and cheeks, "Is it just me, or is this not how orientation is supposed to go?"

I shrugged, but before I could whisper back an answer, Mr. McCully had started to speak again, "Who would like to go first? Don't be shy!"

Nobody moved for a few seconds as everyone looked around to see who would be our sacrificial victim. Then, finally, a boy that definitely wasn't old enough to be a high school student jumped up excitedly, his mop of brown curls bouncing with the movement. His gray eyes shined bright, "Hello! My name is Harley! It's nice to meet you all!"

The kid was maybe ten years old, and I only just came to that realization when Mr. McCully spoke, "Glad to have you here, Harley."

Harley seemed to lose the courage he had to practically shout his introduction and shyly sat back down in his chair. He fiddled with his fingers awkwardly, "Thank you. . ."

Was it possible that the silence felt even more awkward after that? Not because Harley was weird or anything, but I think everyone had the same thought process as me: why was there a kid so young here? Or maybe that was just me thinking those thoughts, and I was the awkward one. Wouldn't be the first time. . .

Well, either way, since nobody volunteered, the Principal made everyone introduce themselves starting to the left of Harley:

I was then introduced to a timid looking girl named Ella, a shorter boy named Warren (don't tell him I called him short. I learned my lesson a long time ago), a boy with black hair and his arms crossed named Ethan, a blonde boy with a charming smile and green eyes named Will, a redhead girl that looks like she could fight every gang in town and win named Adya, another girl that looked like she could equally kick my ass named Kalei, a pair of twins with identical smirks on their faces named Chase and Jake, the boy who had spoken to me earlier named Micah, (me), an excited girl that radiated energy called Layla, a boy that looked like he would rather be *anywhere* else but here named Nolan, another boy that looked like he could be the star quarterback on a football team named Jason, and finally a boy that was from Japan who only moved to the states a few months ago named Ryuma.

God, that was a mouth full. Or, I guess, a paragraph full? Oh, whatever.

Once everyone introduced themselves, Triston got up and dusted off imaginary dirt from his jeans, "Now, with that out of the way, we can finally get the fun part. Everybody up!"

When nobody moved, Triston sighed and almost physically deflated, "Okay, guys, I promise that what's about to happen will be way more exciting than introductions. So have a little faith, okay? Now up! On to your feet!"

We all stood up with different levels of enthusiasm until we followed the principal out of the gym and down the hall. Triston was way too happy-go-lucky as he spoke, "Okay! Now for the tour! And Connor, make sure everything's ready when we get back."

You nodded and headed in the opposite direction, never to be seen again (haha, I wish).

And a tour it was. A very long and very informative tour that lasted more than an hour. Since we were the only ones on campus, the atmosphere was almost eerie as we walked around and took in the sights. The main building, the football field, etc. Finally, we made it back to the central courtyard to stand next to the ridiculously tiny fountain.

I couldn't help but stare. . .in confusion.

In 'what the hell are you doing?'.

In 'is the guy I was on a plane with for five hours *insane?*'.

Because you were waiting for us, your pants rolled up and standing *in the fountain*. And you looked incredibly disinterested as the water soaked the whole left side of your body. . .

"Uhhhh. . ." I said, which was code for: maybe

we should go back to the boat and sail away before it's too late.

Micah leaned closer to me and badly whispered, ". . .what the hell?"

I couldn't help but just shrug helplessly, my code word sadly ignored.

Triston triumphantly stopped in front of the fountain, and with a huge flourish of outstretched arms, he gave us a broad smile. "And that, ladies and gentlemen, ends our tour! Wasn't that exciting? Now, onto the *actual* fun part. Oh, I can't wait! Connor hit it!"

Triston dramatically spun around and pointed at you as if he was a star in a Broadway musical. In response, you let out the most unenthusiastic sigh I have ever heard in my life and uncrossed your arms.

Then you did something that I didn't expect, like, at all.

You raised your right foot and brought it down hard, and there was a loud click, then a bang. You quickly turned around and leaped out of the water before grabbing the Principal and throwing him over your shoulder. Then, you started running away as Triston shouted with a wave, "Have fun, guys! I'll explain in a minute! Promise!"

The ground started to shake violently, and a few of us fell to the ground. Some shouted, some screamed, but that didn't stop the earth from moving. I watched in disbelief as the ground opened up, sliding away from the fountain and towards us. It was so fast that nobody could move in time before we were suspended in the air; a second later, falling and hitting something solid, skidding at an almost 70-degree angle and into a slide.

Screaming was the only thing you could hear as the slide took us farther into the darkness. Everything was a blur of light blue smudges and flailing arms, but it was only a moment before the slide shot me out of the other end. I landed in something scratchy, and I recognized it as a net you might find for performers at a circus. I tried to catch my breath, but it was hard because as person after person flew in the net, it would jostle and send people towards the middle. By the end, we were in a large pile of teenagers, glued together primarily by shock and the force of gravity.

We all laid on the net in complete disbelief before there was a sudden happy yell of joy from the slide, and Triston flew out and into the pile, squishing everyone in the process. You came out seconds after Triston, straight-faced. We shifted and wobbled until the net finally settled...

Then everything was quiet...

Until it wasn't.

"What the hell?!"

"Oh my God, that was awesome!"

"I think I just had a heart attack."

"What kind of school *is* this?"

"I think my life flashed before my eyes."

"Kore wa Amerika no gakkou de karera ga yatte iru kotodesu ka?" (I had Ryuma help me write this. It *roughly* translates to: "Is this what they do in American schools!?")

"What did he just say?"

"I don't know, man. I don't speak Japanese."

"Well, duh, you idiot."

"Wow, bro, I'm wounded."

"Will you guys shut up!?" Nolan yelled in exasperation, slamming his hands down into the net aggressively and causing it to shake. If he could make steam come out of his ears, he would have been a full-on locomotive, with how annoyed he sounded.

The Principal was out of the net and on the floor before we realized he even moved. He probably saw his opening when everyone was shouting. He looked up at us from below, "C'mon, guys. The rope ladder is this way! I promise I'll explain once everyone is down safely!"

I laid there for a moment because my brain felt like I had left it in the courtyard, and my arms shook from adrenaline. I couldn't believe that just happened. I mean, the ground had opened up like we were in an action movie, then the death slide, and now this nutter of a principal had the audacity to be like, 'La La La, this is normal, doo doo doo!'.

I think I needed to update my codeword to say in all caps: WE SHOULD GET TO THE BOAT NOW, THE PRINCIPALS CRAZY!! WEE WOO! WEE WOO! RUN!!

Slowly, everyone started to crawl to the ladder (against our better judgment) and climbed down onto the concrete floor. The last person down was Harley because he was having trouble getting his foot out of the net. Will wandered over and offered a helping hand while everyone else was staring at our future ex-principal, "So, I know that was shocking and all, but I thought it would be more fun this way, don't you think?"

"Are you crazy?" A girl snapped. She had her long black hair tied into a ponytail, and her light blue eyes were fierce. She looked about, ready to smack Triston upside the head, and I racked my brain to try and remember her name before coming up with Kalei.

Kalei, I was already learning just from her demeanor, was a badass.

Triston shook his head, "No, I don't think so? I think one of my five daughters would have noticed if I was."

"You have five daughters?" Harley asked as his feet landed on the ground. Will gave him a look that said, 'that's what you're worried about right now?' but Harley didn't seem to notice.

Nolan, in his brown hair and blue-eyed glory, stepped forward, his hands coming out of his bright red hoodie pockets, "What the hell? Do you think this is okay? Is this even a school, or are you some sick, rich dude that has too much time on his hands and has a thing for kidnapping teenagers?"

Triston sighed, "Maybe I should have just told you all earlier. Sorry. I should have explained this better."

Which wasn't a 'no.' I mean, if I was accused of being a creepy old dude kidnapping people, I might deny it sooner, Triston. Just saying.

Nolan wanted to open his mouth and shout some more, probably, but Triston started talking before he could. An unwise decision going by how

Nolan's face was getting red in anger, "Alright. How to explain? To answer your question, Nolan, yes, this is a real school with real students. Students should be arriving tomorrow to get their dorm assignments and move in for the school year. But you all are *special.*"

Triston then addressed the class at large, "Do you remember what I wrote in the letter about how this year the school was starting a new program?"

Everyone was silent, but a few of us nodded automatically. Triston seemed to be debating with himself before he sighed as he said, "I'll just be blunt. You were all chosen by a lottery to participate in our new program to train vigilantes, that is if you want to, of course."

There it was, out in the air.

The truth of our scholarships and our enrollment.

The truth that no one actually believed.

"You can't be serious," Adya said gruffly from the back of the crowd, her green eyes severe. Then others started to show their lack of belief. Soon, everyone was speaking at once: outrage, confusion, you name it, someone was expressing it.

Triston put up his hands; yeah as if that would calm us down; nice try, buddy, "I know it's hard to believe, but it *is* possible."

32

"But none of us have powers. At least I don't anyway," Micah said next to me, and I nodded in agreement, "I mean, everything you're saying sounds crazy. You do realize that, right?"

"Yet. None of you have powers *yet.*" Triston said, lifting one finger and ignoring Micah's comment, "But what if I told you that I was able to give you some? That I have one myself? Here, I'll show you!"

Triston jogged over and grabbed your arm, dragging you into the fray. And going by your expression, you were enjoying the show before you were so rudely interrupted, "I'll use my power on Connor!"

Triston then loosened his grip and asked you, "Are you alright with that?"

You just shrugged, and Triston turned to face us again, "Okay, so my power is that I can brainwash anyone to do anything. But I don't like to use it maliciously, so. . .I'll just have Connor *dance.*"

Then. . .you started dancing. And my eyes wanted to bleed as I realized the one scary truth about my teacher:

You can't dance to save your life.

"Oh god, make him stop," One of the twins whined. It was Chase, based on the scar that lined the bottom of his right eye, the only thing that helps tell him apart from his brother, ". . .Please?"

I agree with Chase. Please never dance again. Thanks.

"How do we even know if your power," Kalei said as she made air quotes with her fingers during the word 'power,' ". . .is working and that weirdo isn't in on this?"

"Well, I can't just use my power on you! *Stop,*"Triston said, and you halted your horrendous rendition of the Macarena, "How else am I gonna prove it to you?"

Kalei made a face, "Use it on me then. If you have this so-called 'power,' it wouldn't be hard, right?"

And holy shit. Almost everyone in the room was taken aback by how confidently she said that. Like, wow.

Triston faced her fully, but his expression showed hesitation, "Are you sure?"

"Yes," Kalei said with her arms crossed and her stance firm.

"Okay," Triston said as he put his hand on his chin in thought, "Okay. How about. . .this? *Rhyme your sentences.*"

She blinked at him, and we all held our breath in anticipation, "I'm just curious. Do you honestly believe that this is serious?"

Kalei's eyes widened, and some of us let out a gasp of shock, "I didn't mean to say that. Drat! It's as if the words are flowing out of a tap! My mouth needs to cease to flap!"

Kalei slapped her hand over her mouth, and our eyes shifted rapidly between Triston and her in amazement.

"Like, holy shit? She started rhyming!" The other twin, Jake, said, and that pretty much summed up everyone's thought process in two sentences. Doing my job for me, thank you, Jake.

"See? I told you I wasn't lying. So you *can stop rhyming now,*" Tristian said, and Kalei dropped her hand from her mouth, her eyes still looking like they wanted to escape her head from shock.

And, as if the poor boy couldn't hold it in anymore, Harley broke the awed silence by jumping up and down, his eyes sparkling, "That is so cool! Are you saying we can get *superpowers*? Like real, actual powers? Like, I don't know, the ability *to move things with our minds!* Because that would be *awesome!*"

And then the dam broke, and the room exploded with noise as we collectively realized that we could be vigilantes. That there might be a way to get *powers*. Like, *real powers*. I could get x-ray vision, tornados, anything! So now I was on team 'make Triston our principal again' just from the fact the dude *could* be telling the truth. Oh boy, what Alex would give to be there in that moment.

Eventually, Triston put up his hands in a calming gesture, "Okay, okay, I get that you're excited, but I have one more thing I have to say."

The noise died down enough for Triston to speak, but some whispers spilled out occasionally, "Since we're on the subject of powers. . .do you remember that you all had to have your vaccines done before you came to school?"

Everyone nodded, and I subconsciously rubbed my arm at the phantom pain of the shot I had to take a week before.

"Well. . ." Triston looked like he wasn't sure how to say the next part, and I started to get a sinking feeling in my gut, ". . .this is the more. . .morally questionable part in all this, but that wasn't a vaccine."

My feet started to tingle as if they were falling asleep, and I looked down as Triston opened his mouth, "That was the way we gave you your powers. . ."

And as if on cue, I, Skylar Hayes, took to the sky.

I had started floating before Triston had even uttered the word 'powers.'

🌩 Chapter 3 🌩

I want to preface this chapter by saying that a LOT happens, so I'm going to try my best to remember everything. . .also I'm tired, it's 3 in the morning, and I make stupid life decisions.

Carry on.

". . .and they should be kicking in soon. . ." Triston finished lamely as he grabbed my leg to stop me from floating to the ceiling. You know, as if he was a child holding onto a balloon by its string, except the balloon was *me*.

Now, I would love to say that I was calm and collected, the epitome of bravery and coolness, but you would know I was lying, so what's the point? To be honest, I wasn't sure what I was feeling at that moment, as I floated in the air while my entire class stared at me wide-eyed and slack-jawed. Maybe it was shock or a weird collaboration of every emotion, but I didn't fully freak out until I realized one crucial detail about this whole situation:

I was flying, like literally flying, and I had no idea how to get down.

And I didn't even have *time* to process that because Kalei's entire left arm burst into flames.

Kalei screamed, I screamed, and everyone screamed as she shook her arm up and down in panic. And then my feet decided that that was the perfect time to stop tingling, and I fell, bringing Triston down with me. I landed on the hard flooring, and Triston's head landed on my stomach, knocking the breath out of me. I laid there for a moment in a daze, and Triston scrambled to his feet with a hurried 'Sorry!'.

I sat up, grabbed my glasses off the ground, and pushed them on my nose. (I just released I forgot to mention that I lost my contacts, so I was forced to wear my glasses until I got my replacements. Oops, my bad.) My vision came into focus to see that you had walked over to calm the mass of panicked students. The chatter faded out, mainly because Kalei acted less like she was about to die and more astonished that her arms were covered in flames.

Kalei looked up, "It doesn't hurt."

"Well, I would hope not," Triston said as he helped me back on my feet, "It would be awful if you could weld fire and it burned you. Powers aren't usually *that* cruel."

Tell that to my aching butt, I thought bitterly, but it wasn't full-on bitter. I mean, I just got the ability to fly (and yes, I realize my name is now a cheesy pun, thanks a lot, The Universe), but who wouldn't think that was at least a little bit cool? Once you get past the whole 'insert what your power does here' part and the 'I got a superpower, and I'm gonna become a Vigilante' part, it isn't all bad. . .

God, my life is so weird.

Triston tilted his head, "Well, they shouldn't be, but every power is different. Some are harder to control than others. That's why I had all of you come to school early, to try and control the initial. . .uh, manifestation, without *too* much destruction. *Extinguish yourself.*"

Instantly the fire that engulfed Kalei went out, and I wondered why he didn't use his Jedi Mind Trick on me. I mean, I did for all of one second before I was in the air again, and the thought slipped my mind. (I thought about making some sort of wind-related pun here, but I haven't sunk that low. . .yet.)

"Plus, we have no idea what your power is until it shows itself," Triston continued with a smile. At the same time, his hand landed on my shoulder, stopping me from floating any higher. His face became what I would call nostalgic, "I remember when mine manifested. Ah, those were the days. . ."

I saw you roll your eyes, and I wondered how many times you had heard the story. Too many to count, probably. Should I write what Principal McCully told us, or would that be spiteful? Eh, I'll compromise; it had something to do with how he met his wife.

Triston hummed after his long-winded tale of bravery and suaveness, "Well anyway, what I was saying is that we don't know what you'll get until you get it, so. . .that's why I have Connor here. He can, kinda, sorta, see the future."

Harley's eyes lit up, "You can see *the future!?* That's so cool!"

"I can see about a minute or two into the future," You said with a shrug, "The next person to get their power is in a minute and thirty-six seconds. . .ish."

We all waited with bated breath for you to elaborate, but nothing came. You just wanted to watch us sweat, didn't you?

Ella raised her hand after a moment, "Um, Sir?"

Triston smiled kindly at the timid girl in front of him, "Yes, Ella?"

Ella averted her eyes to the floor, and her light brown hair fell a little into her face. Well, as much as it could, seeing as she had tied it up into a braid, "What if we don't want to become vigilantes?. . .I don't know if I. . ."

Triston's smile didn't falter, "Don't worry, Ella, it's not mandatory. If you feel like it isn't for you. . .we could work something out. You can decide to leave, or you can still go to school here if you want, free of charge. . ."

He winced a little and rubbed the back of his neck nervously, letting go of my shoulder in the process, "The only drawback is that we can't undo the powers. . .so, if you do decide to leave, I'll have to brainwash you. Sorry. I have to keep these things a secret. I won't make you do anything, though. I promise."

Triston's smile turned a little sheepish as he continued, "Honestly, I would like for all of you to give this a try, at least a couple of weeks before you decide whether or not to stay."

There was a moment of silence as my class took in the information, standing awkwardly, humming, fidgeting, subdued excitement, and all of that. Not one to be deterred by the silence, Triston looked Ella in the eyes, "I think you would do an amazing job either way. Whatever you decide, don't sell yourself short, 'k?"

"Okay," Ella said unsurely. She still was probably on the fence about the whole thing. And I could tell from some of the other's expressions that they had the same doubts. I can understand that I guess, but by the time I started to fly, I knew my choice.

I mean, who would I be if I *didn't* decide to become a vigilante?

That just wouldn't be me.

I was trying to right myself about a foot above everyone's heads when I saw the next manifestation. At the back of the group, one of the twins, Chase, decided it was the perfect time to suddenly disappear. I was about to say something when the other twin, Jake, turned to the empty air beside him and said, "Oh, we're staying! No doubt. . ."

Jake stared into the nothingness until the disembodied voice of Chase asked, "Why are you looking at me like that?"

"Ten seconds." You said with a sigh.

"Oh. . .my god! That's *awesome!* Bro, you're invisible!"

There was a rustling sound, "I am!?"

"Yeah, dude!"

"Holy shit!"

In Jake's excitement, he somehow hit Chase in the chest; there was a loud 'ow!' and Chase was visible again. And then, in retaliation, Chase hit him back. The moment Chase touched him, there was a small '*pop!*' and so quickly that it was hard to catch, another Jake flew (haha, that didn't last long) out of Jake, blinked, and turned to Chase along with original Jake, "Ow! What the heck, man!"

"Hmm, it seems like there's an echo in here," I heard Triston chuckle, but no one seemed to acknowledge the joke.

A shame, really.

Harley was excited, going by how he whipped his head back and forth with a huge smile. As for everyone else, we all seemed to conclude that this would be a thing now because none of us seemed shocked or surprised by twins suddenly becoming triplets.

Chase turned towards his twin, or, well, both of them, and said, "You know what I'm thinking, right?"

The clones both smirked, "Oh, *this is going to be great*."

Triston hummed as he watched Harley walk over to the twins, who was spouting out a long list of questions, "It's interesting, though, that Identical twins didn't get the same power. I'm glad I decided to enroll Jake as well."

"What do you mean?" Jason asked curiously, his leg bouncing with a nervous tick.

Triston waved him off good-naturedly, "Oh, nothing big. The lottery picked Chase, not his brother. When I saw they were twins, I thought it would be interesting to see if they would both get the same power or not. Plus, I felt guilty that only one twin got t-"

"Triston, the next one is a doozy," You interrupted. Triston nodded as he explained that he had twin daughters and felt it wouldn't be right to leave one of the Solis twins behind.

Well, that was nice of him.

The three Solis brothers high-fived each other, probably finalizing their wicked prank idea with their weird twin telepathy or whatever, when Will suddenly gasped. He fell to the floor, clutching his head in pain. Instantly Triston went into action, running over to Will and kneeling next to him as we all got out of the way, "What's wrong?"

Will looked up with tears pooling at the corner of his eyes and managed to get out, "I

think, ugh. . .I'm. . .reading. . .people's. . .minds. . .maybe?
. . .Oww. . ."

Triston nodded fast and quick, "Ah. *Well, you better stop doing that then.*"

Instantly Will let out a sigh of relief, and Triston patted his shoulder in sympathy, "Were going to need to work on that. Powers involving the mind are tricky. Don't worry. When I first got mine, I kept accidentally brainwashing my wife. I would accidentally make her do the chicken dance and things like that, so don't feel bad."

"Um. . .okay?" Will said with an expression that I can't quite describe, tears still at the edges of his eyes. Maybe he was thinking 'TMI' or something like that. I mean, *I* can't read minds, so it's hard to say.

Also, I would like to point out that I was able to get myself upright with a large amount of concentration. I couldn't quite get myself down to the floor (every time I tried, I would just spin in a circle really fast instead, causing me to almost vomit). Still, I managed to stay about four feet off the ground and keep myself there.

I call that: progress.

And because I had the high ground, I watched as Ryuma started to sink into the floor, "Hey guys,

Yoshida is kinda falling into the ground. . .just to let you know."

Man, it's weird calling Ryuma by his last name. I got so used to calling him Ryu instead. But he wasn't familiar with us at the time, so for now, in dialogue, Yoshida it is. Gotta respect those cultural differences, ". . .Also, Kalei, your hair's on fire."

"Oops, missed one," You said with a shrug when Ryuma was waist-deep in the concrete, and Kalei was furiously patting at a section of her black hair to extinguish her fire.

"How does your power even *work*?" Micah asked, annoyed, as he grabbed onto Ryuma's still solid arms. He tugged and pulled Ryuma out of the ground. Ryu kicked out his see-through legs, and by the third kick, they were solid again. Micah gently lowered him down, and Ryuma thanked him with his heavy Japanese accent, "Thank you, uh. . ."

Micah smiled, "Just Micah's fine, okay?"

Ryuma hummed and went silent. I don't think I saw him say more than a few sentences that first year, now that I think about it. Maybe he was self-conscious about his accent? I'll have to ask him.

Anyway, you shrugged at Micah's question, "It's just kind of a feeling."

I gave you a look, "What does that even mean?"

You then looked me in the eyes and said, "It's like having a feeling that Micah over there is going to suddenly grow a tail in about ten seconds."

"I'm gonna what now?" Micah asked with a look on his face that was genuinely hilarious; it was loaded with so much sass and disbelief. But that soon changed when Micah suddenly had a wolf's tail. It appeared from behind his back with a wag, and I couldn't help but just stare at it.

I jolted when Harley screeched happily and ran over to Micah's tail, grasping it in his hands, "Whoa!"

Micah yelped and jumped away, spinning in a circle as if he were a dog chasing his own tail. Harley had a guilty look in his eyes as he watched Micah grab his new appendage with an opened mouth gasp of shock, "Maybe I should have asked before I touched his tail?"

Jason's laugh was a little strained as he walked over and put his hand on Harley's shoulder, patting it awkwardly, "I don't think that's the problem, Harley."

"I have a tail," Micah said with a squeak to his voice. Warren, who had been silently watching this whole time, walked over and patted Micah on the back in a lame attempt at comfort.

"They're really popping off, huh?" Triston said with a laugh as if a boy growing a tail was natural. But, maybe for him, it was, "I didn't expect so many at once!"

You didn't acknowledge Triston at first. Instead, you raised your pointer finger at Warren and said, "You. Are. Next."

Finished giving your ominous message, you turned to Tristion as if nothing happened and said, "Yeah, I think I like it more this way."

Behind you, Warren's eyes grew to the size of dinner plates, and his hands flew up and off Micah's back. He started to sink, at least that's what I thought at first, but then I realized he was actually shrinking, getting smaller and smaller until he was the size of a soda can. Warren's voice echoed off the walls even with his tiny stature, "You've gotta be kidding me! Damnit!"

Warren was so small I had to squint to make him out as he yelled in rage, punching Micah's shoe in anger. As for Micah himself, he was completely frozen and clutching his tail in a death grip. Probably afraid that if he moved, he would smoosh Warren under his shoes. (A legitimate fear, honestly. I can't tell you how many times I almost murdered Warren over the years. It's practically a long-running joke at this point.)

I saw you stiffen out of the corner of my eye as Ella kneeled next to Micah and stuck out her hand, "Here, I'll help you."

Warren did *not* sound happy about that offer, "Alright, no way in hell I'm doing that. I have some dignity!"

Ella pulled her hand away slowly and bit her lip, "Oh. . .I'm sorry. I didn't mean to. . ."

I couldn't see Warren's expression because he was so small, but I could tell from his voice that he felt guilty, "Uh. . ."

Chase laughed before he marched over with giant exaggerated steps, bending down condescendingly over Warren, "Real smooth, dude, *real smooth.*"

And as if Karma wanted justice on Warren's behalf, Warren shot up like a cap on a bottle of soda that someone put Mentos in and slammed right into Chase's nose. Chase yelped in pain and fell back onto his butt. Meanwhile, Micah jumped out of his skin and bolted away from Warren, his tail between his legs (literally).

And Ella? She just remained crouched, frozen in place, until Warren awkwardly thrust out his hand to her to help her up, "Here."

Warren wouldn't look her in the eyes, his head turned away from her with a faint blush. I got the sudden urge to joke that his 'crush was showing' even though I just met him and knew nothing about his preferences. But I decided not to. (Also, I saw those two coming a mile away...maybe I have your power too?)

Chase groaned from where he was on the floor next to Ella, "I'm fine, thanks for asking...ow..."

"Oh, don't be a baby, I didn't hit you that hard," Warren scoffed as Ella grabbed hold of his hand. He started making the motion to help her up, but instead of Ella getting to her feet, Warren was brought down with so much force that when his head hit the concrete, everyone let out an empathetic *'ooh.'*

Funny how Karma doesn't take sides, huh?

You smiled, like a liar, "Oops. Missed that one too."

Ella scrambled across the floor towards Warren, her hands flying in a panic, "I'm so, so sorry!" Ella cried as Warren held onto his head.

Chase, who was sitting up at this point, turned to Warren mockingly, "Don't be a *baby.* She didn't throw you to the floor *that hard.*"

"Oh, shut up." Warren groaned and gave Chase the middle finger. Chase gasped as if he was scandalized, and Warren just huffed and turned away from him.

Triston clapped his hands, totally ignoring his student's behavior, "Super strength! This is turning out to be an interesting class! I'm glad I decided to spend my money on this."

"Nolan's next."

"What are we, your lab rats?" Nolan glared with his arms crossed aggressively. I mean, he would look intimidating and all, if, you know, he wasn't suddenly glowing like a very scary nightlight. . .Pfft, hahaha.

The room was silent for a moment until we all realized at the same time that Nolan couldn't tell he was glowing like a walking lightbulb. So Jake decided to break the news as tactlessly and bluntly as possible, "Dude, you're glowing."

Nolan blinked, "*Excuse me?*"

His glow seemed to work like a mood ring because the yellow aura around him turned red after Jake's statement. Nolan looked down at his crossed arms, then back up again, "What the hell? No, I'm not. Don't make fun of me."

"Uh. . .yes you are?" Warren said as Ella finally pulled him up in a sitting position. He had a small amount of blood on his forehead, and he wiped it away with the end of his sleeve.

Nolan scoffed, "I'd think I would know if I was glowing. Are you sure you're not concussed, shorty?"

Low blow, Nolan, low blow. Well, not low, like low to the ground or- never mind. Warren's not going to read this anyway. I'm stupid.

Warren's face scrunched up in anger, and he moved to get to his feet with a growl before Layla stepped in, her hands up in the standard 'okay, calm down' gesture, "I can solve this, guys."

She took her phone out of her back pocket and lifted it to take a picture. A few seconds later, she turned her phone around to show Nolan that he was, in fact, glowing, "See? Glowing."

Nolan stared at it for far too long, the gears in his head stalling, struggling to turn. ~~Working so hard to comprehend the simplest of ideas. Struggling to even understand how such a simple concept~~

. . .Nolan just whacked me upside the head.

I'll admit, I kinda deserved that.

Nolan stood there gaping like a fish for a while until he shrugged it off, "Whatever."

Again, it would have had more of a bite to it if he wasn't glowing pink out of embarrassment. I kinda miss the days when he would glow random colors based on his mood. It was fun to get a rise out of him, but now he just lights up when he wants to. Lame.

Triston handed Warren a pink bandaid with flowers on it ("Sorry, it was all I had. Five daughters will do that."), and Warren reluctantly put it on his forehead. Next, Triston rounded up a skittish Micah and told him to 'will his tail away.' Micah blushed scarlet, I laughed internally, and Micah no longer had a tail. It was an exciting couple of minutes, to say the least.

Triston did a mental headcount, "Looks like we only have...four? No, wait, five. I'm surprised, honestly. I didn't think you guys would be so close together."

"Wait...there's more." You said with a sigh, and Triston's eyes lit up with delight.

"Well, alright then!" Triston said with a laugh, "I'll tell you guys what I was going to say in a minute, I guess."

Harley saw his moment and took initiative. He did a little jump and flung out his arms to either side, head tilted up towards the sky, "Powers Activate!"

There was a slight pause as his words echoed, and a few seconds later, after we stared at Harley for far, far too long, there was a sound I could only describe as something breaking concrete. We all spun towards the noise just in time to hear Ethan shout and see that he was getting picked up by a large root coming out of the ground. It was wrapped around his waist like a tentacle from a sci-fi movie and suspended him a few meters above the ground.

Harley threw his arms out in panic as people rushed over to help a struggling Ethan, "Oh my- ah! Powers not Activate! Powers not activate! What have I done!"

Ethan was squeezed harder, and he let out a gasp of, "Stop-gah. . .I can't breathe. . ."

Instantly, as if the root itself was shocked, it let go of Ethan, depositing him on the floor in a heap. The tip of the root nuzzled Ethan's cheek as if it were a dog worried about its master. Ethan swatted it away with a harsh 'get lost,' and it retreated sadly back into the hole it came from.

". . .did that plant just. . .hug him?" Layla asked as Ethan pushed himself up to his feet. He made a face but didn't deny the accusation. He roughly swiped at the dirt that lingered on his clothes, grumbling, "I *hate* plants."

Harley blurted out, "I'm so sorry!"

Ethan stared at him before he sighed, crossing his arms and turning away from Harley's sad eyes, "It's fine. It wasn't your fault anyway. . .I could sense it coming."

"The ability to control plants, I'm guessing," Triston said helpfully.

Ethan made a face but didn't say anything else. Poor dude. Hated plants and dirt, and now his power made him interact with them daily. That's gotta suck. Though I guess not really because I know he likes them now. Exposure therapy at its finest, I guess.

"Hey, bro? Do you want to bet on who goes next?" Chase smirked at his brother casually, as if Ethan wasn't just attacked by a giant plant or anything.

Jake gave him his own smirk in return, "Oh, you're on. Twenty says that she-" Jake pointed at Adya, who scrunched up her face in annoyance before he rethought his decision and spun on the spot to point at Layla instead, ". . . Layla's next! Yep."

"Me?" Layla said in surprise, pointing to herself, her blonde hair bouncing with the tilt of her head, "Oh, I hope so!"

Jason stepped forward with a playful look in his eye, all confidence, "Thirty says I'm next."

"Oh ho!" Chase said as his mouth quirked up, "Mr. Football has entered the fray. Thirty-five on the scary redhead."

"Do you want me to kill you?" Adya growled with a hint of a twitch to her green eyes.

Chase waved her off. Which, I have to say, was very gutsy on his part, "Yeah yeah. Anyone else in on the action?"

You raised your hand, "Can I bet?"

Triston gave you a look that said, 'You should not be gambling with children!' as everyone interested in the bet said, "No!"

"Dude, you can see the future," Chase said, exasperated.

"Ehh, worth a shot. The next one is in thirty seconds. . .ish by the way," You said nonchalantly.

I scooted myself through the air towards the twins, moving my legs back and forth as if I was slipping on ice. Still not able to land but able to move back and forth, I'll get it eventually, "Personally, I think it's Harley."

Even though I had a feeling I would be losing some money, It was worth it just to see Harley's face brighten up as he cheered, "Oh yes, me next!"

"It's a twofer," You offered up helpfully.

"Then, I say it's me! Twenty!" Layla said, all smiles as she jumped up and waved her hand excitedly.

"Are we really doing this right now?" Warren asked in exasperation until his eyes bugged out of his head when Ella spoke up next to him, her hand raised shyly, "I think it's Adya. Um, Ten?"

Triston watched as his underaged students gambled. He smirked, "I agree! Thirty on Adya!"

"Hypocrite." You huffed with a roll of your eyes.

"Wow, what a role model you are," Micah said sarcastically before a smile formed on his lips, "But. . .that doesn't mean I'm not getting in on this! Ten on-!"

Micah's words were drowned out because, as you promised, two people activated their powers simultaneously. Layla took a step forward just as Jason yelped in surprise. Layla surged forth, so fast she was a blur of blonde hair and colorful clothing, and then she was on the other side of the room. She skidded to a stop with a yell of, "I got super speed!"

As for Jason, he had yelped not because he had activated his power. No, he yelled because Adya, next to him, suddenly had a knife sticking out of her elbow.

Jason fumbled over his words, "Adya, your arm there's-knife-!"

Adya Looked down and then brought up her arm, blinking at the foreign object sticking out of it as if this was an everyday thing. She didn't hesitate as she used two fingers to pull the knife out. We all just stared because it didn't leave a mark. There wasn't even a little bit of blood on her skin or a hole where the knife was. Just a normal-looking elbow. She examined the blade before she smirked, "Oh, yeah. I can work with this."

"Within reason," Triston amended with a look in his eyes that said not to mess with his decision. Adya huffed but nodded all the same, looking closer at her new weapon. Adya turned to Chase, casually looking up from her knife, "What was that you said about a scary redhead?"

"Rest in peace," Jake said solemnly, patting Chase's shoulder as he gulped.

"Okay! We have super speed and weapon . . .manifestation? Two more to go." Triston said, changing the subject with grace. He faced the remaining stragglers, "Hey, Connor? Are they gonna appear soon, or can I start showing everyone to the dorm?"

You tilted your head, "I'm not seeing anything for a while."

Triston nodded, "Alright, everyone, follow me. Hopefully, along the way, Jason and Harley will have their powers."

Harley groaned, "Why am I one of the last ones?"

"It could have something to do with how old you are," Triston said as the class started to gather around him, "We haven't used the serum on someone so young. It might just be taking its time?"

"Oh," Harley said glumly, and Jason rubbed his back gently.

Triston pointed to a door on the far side of the room, "That door leads back up to the fountain. That one," Triston pointed to a sturdy set of double doors, "leads to a tunnel that will take you to the back of the island. We have another dock there and a newly built training grounds for you guys."

"That's pretty much it for the school tour! Yay!" Triston opened the door (the fountain one) with a flourish and a smile, "Also. . .I hope you guys like stairs!"

And as we stepped through the doorway and saw the monumental amount of stairs we had to climb, I was so happy that I could fly, "Well, see you guys at the top!"

"Ah, come on, man, how cold!" Chase yelled after me, "You could at least give me a ride!"

"Nope!" I laughed, and Chase yelled out in despair.

I was halfway up when I heard Micah yell, "What do you mean you used up the budget on the slide!"

And I kept on going as if I didn't hear a thing, deciding then and there that I just didn't need to know.

A wise decision, really.

Okay, I'm going to bed.

Bye.

☁ Chapter 4 ☁

I figured out how to stop flying a few minutes after I left the equipment shed. (Nice hiding spot for a secret escape tunnel btw). And then I waited for the rest of my class to finish climbing the stairs of doom.

The first person out was Layla. She had used her speed to slam open the door a minute or two after I had sat down in the grass, but she couldn't seem to stop once she was going. So, now stuck in superspeed mode, she would pass me every so often and send my hair flying with a yell of, "Sooooo clooooooose! Gahhhhhh!" or "Soooooooorrry Skyyyylaaaaarrrr!"

Well, she said more than that, but that doesn't matter.

Layla made another pass, blowing the loose grass I had pulled from the ground out of my hands and into my face. I spat out the lingering greenery from my mouth and sputtered as the door in front of me creaked open, "Please, just figure out how to unstick already!"

I couldn't help but raise an eyebrow when I heard that shout, but it didn't take long before two people flopped out the door and into the dirt, a tangle of limbs.

"You're the one that tried to trip me, so this is your fault!" One of the boys shouted, and I blinked in surprise when I realized that it was Jason. Huh, I thought, he didn't seem like the type to get angry.

The person Jason was struggling to detach himself from groaned, "I said I was sorry, dude! I had to drag your sorry ass all the way up those stairs–!"

"Oh, really–!"

And. . .they were arguing again.

Triston appeared out of the shed with a laugh and jumped over Jason and Chase, who were having a weird sort of tug of war in the grass, "Language, boys."

"When did you ever care about that?" Warren said with an exasperated sigh as he stepped over their flailing bodies with his hands in his pockets.

I got up and wiped the dirt from my jeans before gesturing vaguely to the duo of dorks on the ground. Despite the Principal's warning, they were still letting out muffled curses, "So. . .do I want to know what happened?"

Will was next to emerge to the chaos, laughing awkwardly and side stepping away from the pair not so discreetly, "Jason's power manifested about halfway up the stairs."

"Yeah," Warren said with a roll of his eyes, "And that other idiot got instant Karma. Serves him right."

Well, someone was still salty from earlier.

"I told you I didn't mean to!" Chase pleaded his innocence, and Jason just pouted. Both had stopped struggling and seemed to realize it was useless. I walked over and took a closer look: Jason was stuck onto Chase's side and back, with only one of his legs free. Chase had tripped Jason from what I gathered, and as a result, Jason fell into him, maybe even taking Chase down as he fell. One of Jason's arms was bent at an odd angle, his hand placed on Chase's shoulder as if he tried to push himself away but instead made the situation worse.

"So, his power is that he can stick to stuff? Cool." I said the obvious.

"Yep," Micah chimed in as he and Harley stepped onto the grass, "We tried to pry them apart, but Jason was there to stay."

"You could have tried harder," Both Jason and Chase said at the same time before they both made a sour face and turned their heads away from each other.

"Jinx, you owe me a coke," Jake said flatly, leaning against the doorframe. ("Um . . .that's not how that works. . ." - Harley Thompson, age 10) Jake shook his head at his brother in a show of disappointment.

Another Jake appeared in the doorway and leaned against the opposite side, "Like seriously, wow. I thought I knew you, bro. Such betrayal."

"Get out of the way, or I'll stab you with the weapon I just made," Adya growled behind them. The Jakes jumped before making a hasty retreat to hide behind Will and Micah, who both had exasperation curling on their lips. They shared a look and then promptly sidestepped so that the clones were in full view of Adya.

"No!"

"You guys are so mean!"

"Wow, guys, top ten anime betrayals!"

". . .God dude, that joke is so old."

". . .Get back in my body, you traitor of a clone!"

"Watch out!"

And at that moment, Layla came roaring around the corner and tried to skid to a stop. She finally succeeded but not before running into Jake's clone and poofing him out of existence. She stumbled and fell to her knees before promptly flinging herself onto her back as she took in gulps of air, "Oh god, I'm glad. . .I stopped! I've never. . .run that much . . .in my life!"

"No! Jake 2.0, I didn't mean for you to die like that!" Jake shed realistically fake tears, "He lived such a short life. . .gone in an instant. . ."

"Oh, sorry," Layla said as she slowly sat up, "My bad, didn't mean to kill a dude."

Nolan pinched the bridge of his nose, his hair transitioning through a plethora of different colors because of his annoyance, "Just. . .shut up. Oh my god."

Kalei raised an eyebrow as she stepped outside while Ethan just sighed beside her, looking at the tree next to him with a scowl. A second later, a tree branch inched down to, I assume, tap his shoulder, but Ethan swatted it away with a hiss, "Quit it!"

The branch retreated, and Ethan breathed through his nose as he crossed his arms with an even deeper scowl. Behind him, Ryu stepped into view and went to close the door. Triston instantly perked up when he saw him.

"Alright, now that everyone's here," Triston smiled brightly, turning with a hop in his step, "I shall show you to your humble abodes. Follow me."

And follow him we did, though with varying degrees of pep. (Not before we had to free Ryu's arm from the door. His hand passed through to the other side and immediately went solid. He panicked until Will helped him guide his wrist, which was still mostly ghostly, sideways until it was out. Good job, Will. Thumbs up.) Triston led us past the main building and down a cement path that weaved into a large park/garden area. The trail had one of those poles with multiple signs with arrows to point you where you needed to go. Is there a special name for them? Whatever, it was one of those.

We turned left, where the arrow was pointing the way to the freshman dorms. After a minute or two of walking through different trees, flowers, and the occasional water feature, we arrived at where we would be staying for the foreseeable future. . .

Nestled at the far left corner of the garden stood our four-story dorm. The building had a wrap-around porch with stairs on the front and back. The main entrance was made out of dark mahogany wood, and homey windows lined the bottom floor; I could make out a kitchen and a few couches from outside. There was also a horseshoe pit, picnic benches, and a shed that I assumed held some sort of equipment in it. Finally, behind the building was a swath of trees blocking the view to the rest of the island beyond.

"Say hello to your new dorms," Triston beamed, "I hope you like it."

"Yo, this place is huge!" Chase said as he jogged past Triston and up the steps, peeking into the windows, "I think I see a ping pong table. And. . .yo, is that a DDR machine!?"

Triston nodded, a chuckle on his lips from Chase's excitement, "Yep. On the first floor is a kind of shared communal space: kitchen, laundry, and entertainment. The rest of the floors have your rooms. Girls on the second, boys on the third and fourth."

We all spread out to check out the building as Triston continued to inform us about our living situation, "Your luggage was already brought up to your rooms. You can decorate them however you want. I just ask no inappropriate posters or anything like that. Trust me, I don't want to have that talk with your parents as much as you don't. Other than that, go wild."

"Can we have pets?"

"Yes, as long as nobody is allergic and you clean up after them. You'll have to register them with me first and fill out all the necessary paperwork, but it should be fine with me."

"How about painting the walls? Or ripping out the floor? Making secret passages? Or an inflatable swimming pool?" Jake asked, obviously trying to push some sort of button.

Triston just smiled, "I don't mind as long as you let me approve it first."

"Wha-. . .wait, are you serious?" Jake blinked, slack-jawed.

"Yes."

I'll be honest I stopped listening after that because Layla decided to shout in excitement, 'Well, let's go inside!' and then proceeded to superspeed herself into the main door with a loud crash. She bounced off and flew over the stairs entirely, landing next to me and skidding on the grass with a groan, "Oww. . ."

I couldn't help but let out a laugh before bending down and offering to help her up because, unlike you, I'm a human being with the decency to help people. Thank you very much, "Are you okay?"

Once she was on her feet, she rubbed her side gingerly, "Yeah, haha. Gonna need to work on that, huh?"

Her smile was wide and bright, and I chuckled, "At least you can't accidentally float to space."

"I don't know," Micah said, coming up next to Layla, "It would be cool to visit the I.S.S. At least you don't have cat ears on your head that you can't get rid of."

Layla laughed before reaching over and playing with the said ears. They were the same color as his hair, "I think they're cute! Plus, you could be Ethan right now. . ."

We all turned to Ethan, who was angrily trying to pull his feet off the ground. The grass had wrapped around his shoes, encasing both of his feet, "Would you get off already! Gah, *I hate you!*"

"Yeah. . .you know what? You gotta point there." Micah said, cringing.

She laughed at our classmate's misery, but after the chuckles subsided, she said, "I probably should go help him, huh? Well, see ya later!"

With that, she walked awkwardly and slow, not unlike a robot that needed oil, over to Ethan. He looked very much much like a man who has given up on ever accomplishing his dreams, "Don't worry, I got you! Help is on the way!"

Ethan looked like he might cry as his savior clunkily walked her way over to him, like a true hero.

"Triston, I think you're forgetting something," You said with a suspiciously kind smile as you sat at one of the benches, legs crossed.

"Huh? Oh, that's right! I've got a few more things to tell you before we go inside and get settled." Triston said, and slowly the crowd gathered to listen to what he had to say. "The first is who's in each room. . .and the second is your first official assignment!"

Some groaned (mainly the twins) at the notion of school work, but Triston waved it off good naturally, "Oh, none of that, you're not being graded on it. Connor, do you have the papers?"

You shook your head and got up, "No. I left them on the kitchen counter. I'll be back."

Slouching with your hands in your pockets, you shuffled up the stairs and opened the front door, disappearing inside and leaving it wide open. A few moments later, you came out with a hefty stack of papers. You started passing them out by name.

Once everyone had a packet, Triston started to talk, "Okay, everything you need to know about the school that we haven't covered yet is in here. Your class schedule, a map, how and when you can go to one of the main islands. Also, I know that none of you will read a list of rules and regulations, but we put it in there anyway. As for how we assign roommates. . ."

Chase raised his hand, "Wait, does that mean we don't get our own rooms? I feel like we should have our own rooms."

Triston clapped, "Nice catch! You're right about the first thing. That means everyone will share a room, two in each. And no, before you ask, you can't pick who you room with, and again, no, you can't request to change it either."

At that, there were many groans, and they rose in volume the longer Triston let it fester without saying anything. Eventually, Triston raised his hands in a gesture of goodwill, "Now, now, that's enough. It won't be that bad, I promise. We tried to pair you up with people we think you could get along with. We're not malicious."

"Now, for why you can't change rooms. . ." Triston shrugged, "Part of it is because you will be seeing each other and living together every day anyway. So even though it's cheesy, you'll all have to work together and get along with people you hate. It's how the world works. And honestly, another part is because I had to do it when I was your age, and old habits die hard."

Triston trailed off as if lost in thought. He snapped out of it a moment later, and his pep was back, ". . .but don't worry! You'll have plenty of room to stretch out. Each room is bigger than you guys will need, and if you still don't like the person you're with, well, you can move your furniture as far away as possible!"

There was a long silence, but Triston didn't pay it any mind, "Now, to see who you'll be rooming with for, haha, all four years. . .AHEM, turn to page three."

Hesitantly, people started to flip open their packets to see if they were doomed or not. I scanned the page, past the room number (fourth floor, room 3), and stared at the two words under the roommate section. There, in bold lettering, was my doom:

Roommate:
Nolan Edwards

And before I had time to even contemplate my life choices, Triston decided it was the perfect time to spring one last surprise on us, "Oh, and for the official assignment, it's going to be a year-long project. Well, all four years really. . ."

Triston smiled brightly, "Starting tomorrow, your assignment is to keep your powers a secret from the whole student body! At all times! Or our secret will be out...I know you can do it!"

And as I looked around at my classmates, Ethan still stuck in the grass, Jason's hand glued to the picnic bench, Micah with his cat ears, and Harley for some reason having a staredown with what I thought was a squirrel, I couldn't help but think:

Well, we're screwed.

☁ Chapter 5 ☁

To say that I now hated nightlights was an understatement.

I was envious of Ethan next door, the only one who got his own room. I contemplated how much trouble I would get in if I snuck over and slept in his extra bed. Would it be worth it, I thought, as Nolan shined a bright neon orange in his sleep, lighting up the room as if he had set off a firework.

Sure, I knew he couldn't help it, but if he wasn't such a colossal asshole before we went to sleep, I might have let it slide. But no, he didn't want to room with me as much as I didn't want to room with him; so at least we're on the same page. Mutual hatred is a thing, after all. I scoffed and brought my blankets up higher to block out more of the light.

See Triston: we're bonding!

Ugh.

I turned and snuggled more into the mattress. At least the bed was super comfortable. It was better than the bed I had at home, and even though I had a strange glowing alien named Nolan in my room, I had to admit I was impressed by how big it was. The room, not the bed. Like, you could fit three of my original bedrooms inside. Plenty of room to breathe. And. . .from what I saw on the map earlier, there was even a private beach for everyone to use on campus! I mean, come on, that's cool, and my sister would be super jealous.

I sighed, closed my eyes, and after a while, I started to conk out for the night. Before I fell asleep, I swore I heard someone yell something, but I was already too far gone for it to fully register.

So. . .I guess it'll have to be morning Skylar's problem.

Zzzzz. .

*****

The following day (well, more like closer to noon but whatever), after showering and throwing on some clothes, I found Warren standing on the kitchen counter. He had his arms crossed angrily, muttering, "I just wanted something to drink, dammit. . ."

I wasn't sure if I should go over to talk to him or if it would make him mad to be looked down on—a risky gamble. Oh, he was the size of the glass of water next to him. I should probably mention that.

Luckily, my decision was made for me when Warren made the first move. He spotted me, dropped his arms, and leaned against his glass, the water rippling inside, "Oh, hi, Skylar. How'd you sleep?"

I grimaced, and Warren nodded sagely, "He glowed the whole night, didn't he?"

I let out a huff that turned into a yawn halfway through, "Yeah, like a freaking lighthouse. I have no idea when I fell asleep."

Warren hummed, his expression thoughtful, "Well, I think everyone had a rough night. Micah woke me up in a panic, saying someone had been in our room because he went to use the bathroom, and his hair was bright pink. He thought someone had pranked him or something, and I had to remind him what his power was. That was at, like, two in the morning, I think?"

I winced in the shared sympathy of our sleepless night, "Oof. Well, that sucks. . .where is Micah anyway? Still in your guys' room?" I asked, turning my head to see if I could find him close by.

Warren chuckled, "Outside with Harley. The kid found out what his power was last night. Scared Will half to death."

"Oh, really? What is it?" I said, intrigued.

"I think it would be better if you just see it in action, dude." Warren smiled, "Gotta admit, it's kind of adorable."

I raised an eyebrow because Warren didn't seem the type to call anything adorable, and Warren just scoffed good-naturedly, "Just go look. He's in the back."

"Fine, fine," I said, but as I turned to leave, there was a sound of something cracking, and both of our heads whipped around to see Ella standing at the entrance, a few feet from the door, her eyes wide. In her hand was the door handle, along with a hefty section of the door still attached. She slowly turned to us in mild hysteria, the broken door swaying behind her, "Um. . ."

After a long, *long* silence, I couldn't help myself, and I started cracking up, "Pfft! Oh my god, hahaha!"

Next to me, Warren put his fist up to his mouth as he tried not to laugh. Ella understandably did NOT laugh with us. Still clutching her oopsie in her hand, she squeaked, "Guys, it's not funny! What am I going to do! What if I get expelled! Oh no, I'm gonna get into so much trouble!"

With my voice still hitching with laughter that I tried to smother, I said, "You'll be fine, haha. I'm pretty sure the principal will, pfft, understand. . .hahaha."

Composing himself like a boss, Warren stopped chuckling and said thoughtfully, "I would just go find him and explain what happened. I'm sure he has a way to fix it before everyone shows up later today."

Ah, yes, the other students were arriving around five pm. Which I was kinda grateful for, not gonna lie. We almost had a full day before our class, the walking disaster, had to try to hide our powers. I mean, I just woke up, and Warren is small, and Ella had broken the door with her super-strength. Harley was doing something outside that scared Will half to death, and I had no idea what the twins were up two. . .haha, see what I did there?

So, to summarize, we're going to be the worst kept secret ever.

Ella nodded quickly, and without letting go of her evidence, she dashed out to the building, the broken door swinging in the wind behind her.

"Hmm, maybe I should ask Triston for blackout curtains, you know, so Nolan doesn't wake up the whole damn school." I said once Ella was entirely out of sight and my laughter had subsided.

Warren shrugged, "I mean, it's worth a shot? I didn't see anything, and Micah and I are in the room under you, so maybe you're good?"

"Eh, you're probably right," I said because I was tired and lazy. It was Nolan's problem anyway. Let him suffer the consequences. I pulled my arms up into a stretch, "I'm gonna go see Harley now. Bye."

Warren gave me a salute. As I closed the sliding door behind me, I heard a crash and a curse. Peeking back inside, I saw Warren was big again and lying on the kitchen tile, rubbing his head. His now empty glass of water was spilled next to him on the floor.

I slid the door back open, "You good?"

Warren groaned but waved me off, "I'm fine. Just go."

"Okay, if you say so," I said with a shrug and slid the door shut. Walking across the porch and down the back steps, I looked around for Harley and Micah. I found them about a hundred feet into the forest and surrounded by. . .Oh.

Well, that's. . .

"Yes, I know! I'm glad that I met you too! Oh, don't worry, I'm happy to let you have some!" Harley beamed, and Warren wasn't wrong about Harley being adorable. I mean, c'mon, he was enthusiastically introducing himself to a gathering of cute animals, making sure to give each one the same amount of love and attention; letting them nibble at the bits of food that he held out in his palm. . .

Micah was next to Harley in the grass, and I could tell from his expression that he found it adorable too. His face screamed that he was dying because of the cuteness.

And honestly? Same.

Micah waved when he saw me, his hair now back to its normal color, "Oh, hey Skylar! Look who got his power."

Harley grinned and leaned forward, "I can talk to animals! Isn't that cool!"

A cat with a name tag that read 'Mr. Scruffles' strolled over and rubbed its head against Harley's arm. He reached out and scratched behind its ears. Harley's smile was so infectious that I couldn't stop myself as a smile of my own pulled at my lips, "Oh yeah, that's super cool."

"I know, right!" Harley laughed, and some of the animals shifted happily next to him.

Oh god, cuteness overload.

I'm dead.

"I guess it was worth the wait, huh?" I said brightly.

"Yeah, I got it last night. . ." Harley's expression fell a bit as he started to look guilty, ". . .I didn't mean to scare him. Do you think he'll forgive me?"

It took me a second to realize he must have been talking about Will. Micah reached over to ruffle Harley's curly hair, "Oh, trust me, he already forgave you."

"Really?"

"Yep."

"Oh, that's a relief." Harley sighed before he seemed to move on from his plight, turning excitedly back to his animal friends, "Did you hear that? He forgives me!"

Micah's face was soft and also a bit reluctant when he said, "Anyway. . .it was fun hanging out with you, Harley, but I think I should go. Thank you for introducing me to everyone."

"Okay," Harley waved without looking away from his new friends, "See you later!"

Micah got to his feet and waded through the crowd. Once he was next to me, I teased, "So. . .I heard you had a fun night."

Micah groaned in embarrassment. I took pity on him, "Don't feel bad. At least you weren't up all night with your own personal light show."

Micah blew a sympathetic wave of air out of his mouth as we started to climb the back stairs of the porch, "That sucks."

I shrugged, "Just gotta get used to it, I guess. Though it doesn't help that the turd is still asleep upstairs. Whatever. I'm more curious about what happened to Will."

Micah laughed as we rounded the corner, heading to the front of the building. I wasn't sure why we didn't just go through the back door, but I let Micah guide me along, too focused on our conversion to care, "Oh, that's a story right there. Harley woke up to noises from outside and opened the door to his balcony. Will woke up in the middle of the night to a colony of bats in his room, freaked, and ran out of his dorm screaming at three o'clock in the morning."

I let out a loud laugh, "Warren wasn't kidding when he said everyone was having a rough night!"

Micah's chuckle was only a bit strained, "First, I woke him up like a maniac panicking over pink hair, and then Will was screeching outside our room thirty minutes later. Which, by the way, also woke up Jason and Yoshida. So yeah, I would say we had a rough first night in the dorms."

"You know what? I take it back. I'll take the Nolan nightlight any day."

Micah snorted.

"What's so funny?"

"AHH!" Micah and I both jumped out of our skins as Ryuma appeared out of nowhere beside us, his whole body transparent. He just blinked at our reaction and didn't say anything.

"Jesus, you scared the crap out of me!" I said as I tried to keep my heart in my chest. Micah wasn't much better, his words coming out with a slight rasp, "Yoshida, no offense, but where did you *come from?*"

Ryu blinked again, "I walked through the wall."

Well, I mean, okay.

But more importantly: "Hey, wait, why aren't you sinking?"

"I float," Ryuma shrugged as if that explained everything. Which, I guess, it kind of did. I looked closer, and low and behold, he was floating a few inches off the ground.

"Huh," I said in wonder.

Micah straightened up once he recovered from his heart attack, a frown of thought on his face, ". . .that's weird. Maybe it's because you are fully transparent? Like, you have no weight pulling you down, gravity-wise? Or maybe it's a subconscious thing?"

Ryuma stared for a second before he became solid and hit the porch with a light thud as his feet made contact, ". . .Micah, you never answered. What was funny?"

Micah's brain seemed to stop for a second as he processed the sudden change of subject, "Huh? Oh, uh, I laughed at something Skylar said. . ."

Ryuma averted his eyes shyly, "Okay."

And then, without looking up or saying anything else, he walked back through the wall and into the dorms beyond. There was a moment of silence until I turned to Micah, "Well, that was a thing. . ."

"Nah, I think he's just socially awkward," Micah said with a shrug.

"Hmm. . ."

"Hey. . .how do you think he learned how to control his power so fast?" Micah asked after the pause went on for a little too long, "Do you think he practiced last night?"

I gave Micah a look as I started to rise into the air on accident, like the universe had perfect comedic timing, "How would I know?"

Micah opened his mouth, watched me grab onto the railing so I didn't fly into the sky, then blew a bit of air out of his mouth, "Okay, point taken."

I started walking along the railing with my arms, my feet in the air, before I turned to Micah in defeat, "Hey. . .can you help me get back inside? Please? Before I lose my grip?"

Micah's lips twitched as if he was holding in a laugh, but he hid it pretty well as he nodded, "Sure thing, bud."

". . .Thank you . . ."

"No problem. . .what the heck happened to the door?"

"Ella."

"Ah."

*****

Layla was killing it on the DDR machine when you walked in around four in the afternoon. You didn't bat an eye at the broken front door or the fact that Jason was stuck to the ceiling like a discount spiderman (it's a long story and my hand's getting tired. Deal with it). Instead, you pulled out the megaphone that you were hiding behind your back, and we just watched with varying levels of 'wtf' on our faces.

The megaphone squealed as you turned it on and everyone in the room grimaced, "You should be on the first floor in five minutes, or you'll get a week's worth of detention!"

Without turning it off, you threw the megaphone on the kitchen counter, took a seat on one of the stools, and crossed your arms. The six of us who were just chillin' on the couch looked at each other before Will, bless his heart, turned to you with a tilt of his head, "Um, what's going on?"

Your expression shifted through a variety of emotions before it settled on a wide grin, "You'll find out once everyone's here. Be patient."

"Should we be worried?" Harley very loudly stage-whispered to Will.

"Probably," Jason said calmly from above us.

Once the words left Jason's mouth, you got up from your chair, grabbed three large couch cushions, haphazardly lined them up underneath Jason, and then went back to your stool as if nothing happened. You only let out a brief warning, "Brace yourself."

Jason blinked before he suddenly let out a yelp as his sticky powers turned off, and he fell to the floor and onto the cushions with a thump. He groaned and rolled over, "Ow."

"You're welcome."

". . .thanks, I guess," Jason said, his voice muffled by the couch cushion.

After that, we waited as the rest of the class made their way downstairs one by one. The most exciting ones were Ryuma, who fell through the ceiling and landed in the armchair, making everyone jump, and the twins, who loudly thudded down the stairs at the last second with loud shouts of 'Hurry up!' and 'Do you want detention!?'

They got detention, the fools.

"That's not fair," Jake said glumly as he flopped on the floor in front of one of the couches. Chase nodded regretfully as he sat next to his twin. I decided not to comment that Chase didn't have a scar under his eye or the fact that I saw 'the real ones' outside the window sneaking into the forest behind you.

It just seemed more fun that way.

Harley opened his mouth, and I thought that the twin's master plan would be foiled then and there, but he just asked, "What's going on?"

You lifted yourself from your stool with a grunt and surveyed the room, "We're going to do a fun little exercise. Far away from the rest of the student body. Think of it as training for tomorrow. Follow me."

Giving none of us time to question where the heck we were going or what the exercise was, you marched to the backdoor and slid it open with a swish, and disappeared outside.

Nobody moved. Because, seriously, why would we? The last time we had to ride a death slide and thought that maybe we were being kidnapped. So, yeah, a little hesitancy on our part is understandable. After a minute, you stuck your head back inside, irritated, "Well, get a move on! We don't have all day! People are going to show up soon."

Nolan pushed himself up with a scowl and a huff, crossing his arms. Reluctantly, people followed his lead and got up too, filling out the back door and onto the lawn.

Once we were all outside, you gestured to the path leading into the trees, "Follow this trail until you are out of the forest. I'll be waiting for you on the other side."

"Wait, you're not coming with us?" Layla, the one who asks all the right questions, said.

"Don't worry, it won't take you *that* long to get there. You'll be fine."

Well. . .that's totally not suspicious or anything. . .

"Alright. Good luck, and I'll see you soon," You turned away with a wave, dodging all our questioning looks with grace.

"What the hell? Get back here!" Nolan shouted as he seethed, glowing a deep red. And. . .You just kept walking because, of course, you would.

"Don't ignore me!" Nolan growled, furious.

"We're totally about to get murdered in the woods, aren't we?" Micah deadpanned as you disappeared in the distance.

"Whatever. I'm not scared of some dumb trees." Adya said gruffly as she turned and marched down the path, "See ya, losers."

"That's coming from the girl that can literally pull a weapon out of her ass," the fake Chase grumbled. But that didn't stop him from following her all the same, his twin not far behind. The three of them disappeared, and Kalei shrugged, turned around, and followed them.

Harley grinned as he went next, skipping past us and down the path, "It's okay, guys! My friends will help us if we are in trouble!"

He disappeared around a bend, and Ethan made a face of pure regret, "I don't want to go in there. . .there's so many. . ."

"Let's just get it over with then." Warren lamented. He jogged over, grabbed the hood of Ethan's jacket, and pulled him toward the trees. Ethan struggled out a 'Please no!' but Warren didn't let go, and the two disappeared down the path with a few more strangled yells of distress. . .

(Poor Ethan.)

After that, everyone left decided that it ultimately wasn't worth worrying about and started walking. Nolan grumbled angrily from the back, and we eventually caught up with the others. The walk was pretty much uneventful other than the few times someone's power suddenly popped off, and we had to do an impromptu rescue mission.

Ella wiped the sweat from her forehead, "Um, how long have we been walking?"

"Yeah," Jake said as we went up another zig, leaving the zag behind us, "It feels like we've been at this forever."

"And why is-," Micah gasped for air, ". . .it all uphill?"

"It has to have been more than an hour, right?" I said as I shamelessly held onto Micah's shoulders as I floated behind him, "'Won't take long,' my ass."

"Here she comes again," Warren warned as Layla flew past us, leaving a dust cloud in her wake. I gripped Micah's shoulder harder, so I didn't fly off into the sun, and he grunted at the sudden weight.

"Sorry."

"I wasssss sooooo clossssseee!" Layla"s shout sounded in the distance. By that point, she was already completely out of sight.

Jason coughed up dust, "At least she made a breeze?"

"Can confirm," Will said with a tired sigh as he put his phone away, "It's been over an hour."

"Ugh," Fake Chase said, "Why do the clones have to deal with this?"

"Um, way to blow our cover, dude," Clone Jake said, but he didn't look all that upset about it. He grabbed the front of his shirt and started to fan himself.

"I don't care. We should go on strike."

"Clone labor union?"

"Clone labor union."

"If he knew how long this would be, he could have at least let us change into shorts or something. Damn, it's hot," Warren said, irritated and ignoring the 'twins.' He rolled up his sleeves to get some relief from the heat.

"Come on, guys, it's not that bad," Kalei said, not even close to winded and still wearing her black hoodie. Her fortitude will never be matched. (Also, it might have something to do with her withstanding fire? That's my theory anyway.)

"Gloria says we're almost at the top," Harley put in as he petted 'Gloria' where she was perched on his shoulder.

"What is that? A squirrel?" 'Chase' asked, peering over Jake's shoulder to get a better look.

"I think it's a mongoose." Will replied tiredly, "Hawaii doesn't have squirrels."

"Wait, is that true?"

"Does it matter!?" Nolan yelled, annoyed. Gloria jumped off Harley's shoulder in alarm and ran into the woods.

Harley gasped, "Wait, Gloria, don't go! Nolan, why did you do that to her?"

Nolan paused for all of one second of regret before he scowled, pushing past us and up the trail. Harley's face scrunched up and went to follow him, but it was Warren who stopped him with a shake of his head, "Let him go. It's not worth it."

After that, the walk had a tense air to it, and there wasn't much talking, a little bit because of Nolan's hostility but mainly from the lack of actual breath. Once we got to the top of the hill and started making our way back down, Layla finally stopped running, and I managed to quit floating. (Thank you, Micah, my good friend, for carrying me so far. I appreciate you!) It was at least another twenty minutes until we made it to the bottom, where you waited for us with a smile on your face, "Have a nice walk?"

We were all so irritated/tired that we just gave you the silent treatment. You snickered, "Sorry about that?"

"You don't look sorry at all, you jerk." It was surprisingly Ethan who spoke up. He had a bunch of leaves in his hair and looked extra irritated. Way too many trees wanted to hug him on the way here. It was a struggle for everyone.

"Oh, don't be like that," You said as you opened the cooler next to you on the ground, "I'm just getting you ready for what's to come."

"What. . .do you mean?" Jason asked warily. Yoshida was leaning against his shoulder, his eyes half-closed and sweat beading his forehead.

"Who wants something to drink?" You dodged the question, and when nobody moved, you sighed, "Okay, okay, fine."

"That," You got up from your crouch and swiped dirt off your pants, gesturing behind us, ". . .is what Triston and I call the 'Walk of Champions.' It's how you'll be getting to your training every day. And before you complain, it was Triston's idea."

Uh-huh.

It was totally Triston's idea.

Yep.

"Think of it as part of your training. After a while, that 'Walk of Champions' will be nothing for you guys. Plus, it's a bonus that the path doesn't go anywhere near the other students, so all you have to do is sneak away unnoticed. *Now,* does anybody want a drink? You might want it before the exercise."

"Wait. The 'walk of doom' wasn't the 'exercise,'" Jake said as if it was an outrageous scandal.

"Nope." You said cheerily, having no intention of correcting Jake, which spoke volumes, "The real exercise takes place over there."

You pointed to one of the multiple buildings in the clearing. This one was painted a pale white with orange accents, and lining the top were large windows. Unfortunately, they were more for letting in the sun than to look through, giving us no insight into what was lurking inside.

"Do I want to ask what this 'exercise' is?" Micah sighed as he gave up the standoff and reached into the cooler for a bottle of water.

You grinned, "Are you guys ready for what I call 'The Dodgeball Game from Hell'? Because I sure am!"

☁ Chapter 6 ☁

I'm gonna skip ahead a bit since I want to get to the good part. Here's a quick summary:

We got mad, complained some more about how you are a terrible human being, and that you can royally suck it. Nolan was the angriest, Adya the most excited, and eventually, we all ended up exactly where you wanted us: about to play the Dodgeball Game from Hell.

Also, the building was just a typical gym. I don't know what I was expecting, honestly.

"So, the rules are simple," You smiled, and I have to say that it was probably the most genuine look of joy I've ever seen on your face, "You'll be split into two teams. If you get hit by the ball, you're out. If you catch the ball, the other person is out, and you can bring someone from your team back in. The most important rule is. . .powers are fair game.

Use them however you want. Or don't. I don't care either way."

You started walking backward, towards the bleachers behind you, "Start choosing your teams; you got three minutes. The winning team will get a special prize, so choose wisely!"

Nobody moved.

You sat down on the top bleacher and took out your phone. You gave us a look after a moment of awkward silence, "What are you waiting for? You got two minutes and twenty-five, four seconds left. Whoever isn't on a team when times up has to write a fifteen-page paper about time management."

. . .You're evil, you know that?

"Nah, man, I'm so not down for that," 'Jake' and 'Chase' said at the same time before scrambling to one side of the court, "Team number one over here!"

"Why would we be on your team?" Micah asked. It wasn't harsh, just brutally realistic, "Once you get hit, both of you will just disappear, right? Poof."

"Shhh," 'Chase' said, "Teach, doesn't know that yet!"

Adya cracked her neck and walked over to the twins, "Whatever, I'll make up for the both of them."

"Hell yeah!" 'Chase' raised his hand for a high five, but Adya just walked past him without even raising her hand an inch, "Okay, no high fives, got it."

Warren stepped over the line and onto the other side of the court, "Guess I'll start the other team."

After that, everyone just kinda shifted until they were on one team or the other. The last person to choose was Nolan. And I didn't think he was going to do anything until you said nonchalantly, "I'm looking forward to reading that paper, Nolan~."

Nolan huffed, marched over to the side I was on, and crossed his arms, joining my team.

So, in the end, we were split up like this:

Team 1	Team 2
Warren	Jake & Chase
Ella	Harley
Me	Adya
Layla	Will
Ryu	Ethan
Micah	Kalei
Nolan	Jason

You got up, put your phone in your pocket, "Alright, let's get this started. I'll be right back."

You headed to the closed door at the back of the gym, opened it, and then disappeared inside. We all waited, and in the silence, Layla spoke up:

"I meant to ask. . .what's with the penguin hair clip?" Layla asked as she gestured to the object nestled in Will's hair.

Will blinked from the other side of the court, "Huh?"

Layla tapped her temple, "Your hairclip. Where'd you get it?"

"Oh." Will chuckled, reflexively reaching up to his head, "I got it from Triston. Apparently, his daughter can also read minds, and he made these for her to control it."

"Why a penguin, though?" Harley asked, and Layla did a fantastic job imitating a bobblehead with how fast she nodded.

"He let me choose a few that she said I could borrow. She has a thing for animals. I picked the ones I liked the most out of what she had," Will raised his hand, putting up a finger one after another, "I chose the kangaroo, turtle, penguin, and cat ones."

"What were the other options?" I asked, curious.

"An octopus, elephant, and a dog. Triston said he would have some other ones made for me, but it'll take about a week until they're done."

"How do they work?" Warren asked, now invested in the conversion too, "Do they like, I don't know, block brain waves or something?"

Will shrugged with a grimace, "I'm not sure, honestly. But if they help with not making my head feel like it's gonna explode, I don't care how they work."

Some of us sympathetically hummed our agreement. Then the conversation lulled, and we were left just staring awkwardly at each other until:

"Alright!" Your voice echoed around us in the gym, "Fair warning, I'm about to drop the balls. If any of them hit you, you're automatically out. The game starts in. . .five. . ."

Everyone tensed like a deer caught in headlights.

"Where *is* he?" Jason asked, looking around the room, subconsciously bringing his arms towards him in a ready-to-go stance.

"Four. . ."

Warily, Warren tilted his head, so he was staring at the ceiling, "He said drop but. . . from where? ("Three. . .") I don't see anything. . . "

"Two. . . "

Everyone held their breath, and you waited for more than five seconds for dramatic effect. In that time, Warren was able to get out, "Hey, guys, I think we should move-"

"ONE!"

And then the sky fell.

Dun dun dun!!

In all seriousness, though, you must have hit a switch or something, and part of the ceiling retracted into itself. And then came the ball armageddon. Like, you could play that song that goes DUN DUN DUN DUN, and it would match perfectly as the balls started to rain down around us. People screamed as they dodged out of the way, running to the relative safety of the bleachers, and I could hear your laughter echoing around the gym, eerily manic. The balls hit the floor, all at once, and it caused a whole other problem as they bounced, going in every direction and some straight towards us.

"AHHHHHHHHHH!"

"Hit the deck!" Jason yelled as he practically dived behind one of the bleachers. Harley squeaked and covered his face as the balls heading his way flew past him and hit the wall behind him. (Thinking back, that was the first time Harley showed off his unbelievably good luck. A start of a legacy.) Ryuma made his legs translucent and sunk through the floor to dodge, bracing himself with his arms. Nolan braved the wave, subsequently getting hit with six balls at once before sitting down; he didn't even try to get out of the way.

A great teammate, am I right?

HA.

Then, fire activated in Kalei's hands, making her let out a gasp of surprise and almost setting my clothes on fire, "Oops! I'm sorry!"

Kalei tried to shake her arms to put out the flames, and everyone around her frantically stumbled away. She kind of looked like those guys that spin fire around at la'au's. What are they called again? Aren't they just called fire dancers? I'll look it up later. (I was right, btw.)

'Chase' dove away from Kalei's flailing arms but ended up right into the line of fire (haha). 'Jake' yelled as his partner in crime was hit by a ball straight into his back. POOF! And then 'Chase' was gone.

You shall be missed.

"I'm gonna forget for now that Chase. . Jake? Whatever. One of them just disappeared, but what are you guys waiting for? GO! GO! GO!" You delightfully encouraged.

"Okay!" Adya yelled as she bent down to grab the ball closest to her. She had the biggest grin of happiness on her face as she pulled back her arm to throw, "Take this!"

Ella yelped as she ducked out of the way, the ball sailing over her head and straight at Micah, scaring the freckles straight off his face, literally. He dodged in the nick of time, "Ahh! What the hell, Adya!"

"Hey, we're in a battle, wolf boy."

"Wolf boy? Seriously? Also, this isn't a batt-OOF!" Micah gasped as another ball came his way, hitting him solidly in the chest. Micah seemed to freeze on the spot, his breath knocked out of him, and then he went down. And. . .the freckles were back.

"Oh, you wanna play that game, huh!" Warren growled though I could see the smirk at the corner of his mouth as he started throwing his ammunition back at Adya. She dodged with expert skill and scrambled off the bleachers and onto the gym's floor. She picked up three more balls and threw them at Warren with FAR too much gusto, the last one sweeping past Warren's nose as he leaned to the side to get out of the way.

Adya let out a massive breath, "Hah, you think you can hit me!"

"Oh, now it's on! Take this!" Warren yelled as he jumped off the bleachers and flung his ball at a grinning Adya with a wild sidearm throw.

She dodged easily.

"Okay! Both of you are enjoying this way too much!" Jason said as he struggled to get up from his hiding place. Every time he went to stand up, he seemed to snap back down like his body was a rubber band. Stuck to the floor by his own power, yikes.

Well, I thought, easy target, right?

"Sorry, dude," I said as I walked over to Jason, dodging a stray ball from the previous duo's intense 'battle.' I kneeled down and gently pressed the ball in my hand against his shoulder, "No hard feelings?"

"It's fine," Jason sighed dejectedly, then, "Holy shit! Watch out!"

Jason reached up as best he could and grabbed the front of my shirt, yanking me down next to him as two FLAMING BALLS of DEATH flew over my head in a streak of red and orange. I could feel the heat singe my hair as they passed, and I looked at Kalei in shock, with my glasses falling half off my face. She stared back with a slight gap to her lips before a mischievous smile ran across her cheeks, "Oh, that was awesome."

I got to my feet, making sure not to accidentally step on Jason. He looked absolutely terrified by Kalei and was trying harder to get unstuck from the floor. I adjusted my glasses, "What the heck! Are you trying to burn this place down!?"

Her grin only showed more teeth as she grabbed the closest ball, setting it aflame instantly. The smell of burnt rubber overtook my nose, "Eh, he said powers were fair game, right?'

"Yep! Go wild!" You confirmed from wherever the hell you were. Even though I couldn't see you, I could hear that stupid smile in your voice.

In front of me, Kalei readied another ball, and all I could say was: "Well, shit."

Kalei just smiled sweetly with fire in her eyes (. . .) and chucked her molten dodgeball. At the last second, I managed to activate my power, the ball almost setting my laces into an inferno.

I instantly regretted the decision when my flight decided it was the perfect time to take me on a rollercoaster ride across the gym. It spun me like a top over everyone's heads, making me look like a crazy ballerina. My glasses flew off my face and into the unknown, making everything even more blurry than it already was. It didn't help that Harley hadn't moved an inch and was laughing his ten-year-old ass off at my misery, pointing at me like I was a rogue kite in a hurricane.

Pro: I became the ultimate dodgeball master.

Con: I was SO going to throw up.

Putting a mental foot down, I spun to an abrupt stop in the middle of the gym, close to the ceiling. My hands flew up to my lips as I tried not to hurl. Swallowing down the bile in my throat, I glanced down to see the utter chaos that was the Dodgeball Game from Hell, squinting to make it all out:

Everyone was throwing balls at each other with no care of sides or boundaries, climbing on the bleachers, hiding behind doors, and powers activating willy nilly. The people who were already out weren't sure where to go now that they weren't in the game anymore and just tried not to get hit again. (Jason was still stuck, and I kinda feared for his life). Part of the gym's floor was slightly smoldering from Kalei's demon balls, and Ella accidentally sent a ball straight through the side of the building, sheetrock and all, and took a nice chunk out of a tree outside. Layla dodged with her superspeed and proceeded to run straight into a wall, hitting it with a thud, letting out a laugh (and a yelp of pain). Even Nolan was panicking as he tried not to DIE, even though he was out of the game from the beginning.

Utter Chaos, like I said.

But. . .it also looked like a lot of fun.

Against any sort of survival instinct, I decided to be my very best version of Peter Pan. I tried to angle my flight so that I was back in the game. (You know, once I was sure I wasn't going to upchuck all over everyone. Because I knew they would never let *that one* go). I was maybe 75% successful, my body wobbling and jerking slightly in the air. Still, I was proud when I managed to catch a ball that was hurtling towards me, courtesy of Adya. I flew back a few inches from the impact but smirked at her as she spewed out a few curses. She then joined the cluster of students that were out.

"Good job, man!" Warren shouted as he ran back into the battlefield, deciding for himself to be the one to go back into the game. Everyone sort of paused as we waited for him to get back in, all sportsmanship-like.

I did a mental headcount of who was still in the game, noticing that the class was already cut in half, with fewer of my teammates still in. Only Warren, Ella, and I were left while the other team still had Harley, Ethan, Kalei, and surprisingly the clone of Jake. Did seriously no one manage to hit him this whole time? Really, no poof? I was honestly impressed by that twin's dodgeball skills.

There was a weird sort of standoff as we stared at each other from different sides of the court. Harley looked like this was the best day of life, all bright eyes, and a shining smile. (God, that kid.) Ethan had this expression that I couldn't quite place, uncomfortable, maybe? Kalei's fire had turned an intense but really cool blue, and she eyed the ball closest to her. . .that was rolling into the middle of the group like those tumbleweeds you see in western movies. Everyone's eyes shifted to watch as it came to a stop. The exact same distance between both teams.

A pause, then:

"What the hell are you guys doing! Hurry up and chuck things at each other!" Adya yelled from the sidelines, throwing her hands up as if someone had just scored a goal in a soccer game. Nolan pinched the bridge of his nose with a long sigh while Micah looked like he was trying not to laugh.

And that's when Ryu made the most stunning appearance in the Dodgeball Game from Hell's history. Faster than my eyes could fully catch, he flew out of the ground and grabbed the ball. Solidifying only his hand, he sunk down, and the ball traveled across the floor, held by his disembodied hand. He reappeared in front of a startled Ethan and shoved the ball roughly into his chest. A satisfying 'oof!' came out, and Ryuma sank through the floor again.

Instantly the game restarted in a flurry of motion. Kalei reached down to the ball Ryuma just dropped and chucked it with all her strength. I flew backward, Ella sank to the floor in terror, and Warren let out a war cry as he ran to one of the many piles of ammunition on the floor. Ethan fell onto his butt, and Kalei's eyes lit up as she ran to get more Ammo. Jake scrambled but wasn't fast enough to escape as Ryu appeared behind him and jabbed his shoulder harshly with his hand. Jake disappeared into a puff of smoke with a perfectly cut-off scream.

"Yo! Go Ryuma!" Layla cheered from the sidelines. Ryuma blushed lightly at the use of his first name but was focused enough to dodge an attack from Kalei.

"That ain't legal, Teach!" Adya screamed in outrage.

"Eh, I'll allow it."

"What!? Bullshit!"

"Wait, what's going on?" Jason's voice rose from the bleachers, "I can't see anything!"

I don't know if anyone answered Jason; I was too focused on not getting hit as Harley aimed at me. His innocent smile morphed into something more devious (read: evil) as he sprinted around the gym. He sent all of his balls my way, "This the best day of my life!"

And you'd think that a ten-year-old wouldn't have that much accuracy or throwing power, but damn, does that kid have an arm on him. No wonder he tried out for baseball and made the team so young.

Meanwhile, Warren and Kalei were in a very intense head-to-head battle. Both equality trying to get each other out. One after another, flaming balls flew through the air, and Warren dodged with an aggressive counterattack of his own. Ryu appeared at random to disrupt the flow, but in the end, Kalei hit him with a miraculous (and accidental) shot to his solidified arm as he went to pick up a ball.

The others on the sidelines were eating up the action, and the cheering got louder as the match went on:

"You got this, Warren!"

"Yoshida, you were so cool!"

"C'mon, guys, please just tell me what's going on! Ah, man, I'm missing everything!"

(Poor Jason.)

"Get him, Harley! Take him down!"

"That was a good try, Ella!"

"Oh god! Is he gonna hurl?"

The last one was about me as I landed roughly in front of Ella, one too many spins in the air making me gag. Stumbling forward on weak legs, I quickly put both hands over my mouth in an attempt not to lose everything in my stomach. Kalei saw my weakness for what it was and decided to abandon her crusade against Warren and take aim at me instead.

"Oh, no, you don't!" Warren yelled as he lifted his arm to throw, but then his eyes widened, "Shit!"

With a pop, he was suddenly tiny. The ball he was holding fell to the floor and almost squashed him. He lept away just in time, but that didn't stop the flaming ball of terror that was on course to take me out. I moved to dodge when I heard Ella yell out behind me, "H-here goes nothing! T-take t-this!"

BAM!

I fell to the floor clutching the back of my head, my vision swimming and getting dark on the edges. I couldn't figure out what had just happened, and multiple sets of feet ran towards me with a few yells of 'are you okay!' and 'That had to hurt!'. I barely heard Ella as I slumped against the floor in pain, "Oh my god! Skylar, I'm so sorry! I swear I didn't mean to hit you!"

"Guys! What happened? C'mon please tell me!" Jason's warbled yell was far away.

And then I was gone, lost to unconsciousness.

I went down in my first Dodgeball Game from Hell because of friendly fire.

God, my head hurts just thinking about it.

☁ Chapter 7 ☁

I woke up with a raging headache.

Like, oh-my-god-this-is-the-worst-thing-to-happen-to-me-I'm-gonna-dieeeeeee kind of headache. It felt like it took me forever to get my bearings, but eventually, I figured out that I must be in the nurse's office. I was lying on one of the three beds in the room, the privacy curtain pulled open and still in my clothes from the dodgeball game. Though, someone had pulled off my shoes and set them against the wall near my bed.

'Ugh, what *happened?*' I groggily asked the ceiling.

It didn't answer back.

Not that I expected it to. I'm not that crazy. I blinked back that thought and tried to remember how I got there, subconsciously wiggling my toes in my socks.

Okay, so there was the Walk of Doom . . . .the game, Kalei aiming. . . .

Oh yeah, Ella hit me in the back of the head.

With her super-strength.

Hard.

Ow.

Distantly, I heard the sound of rustling paper over my groan of pain, "Oh, you're awake. How are you feeling?"

"Huh?" I said dumbly. It came out more like, "Ugh?"

"Haha, yeeaaah, I expected that answer."

I hissed as I moved to see who had talked. On the other side of the room, sitting down in a rolling office chair and wearing scrubs, was a man with curly brown hair, green eyes, and a gentle smile. He looked like he was in his late twenties or early thirties.

"Um . . .?" I replied in confusion.

He got up from his chair and set down the papers he held on his desk. Weaving past the other two beds and coming to my side, he put his hand on my forehead. Huh, my brain processed. . .is his hand glowing. . . blue? Oh, and he has a beauty mark right under his left eye. Or at least I thought he did; my vision was a little blurry. That's when I remembered that my glasses were long gone, lost in the void known as the Dodgeball game from Hell.

The nurse hummed above me, "Well, your head is mostly healed, but it's going to ache a little bit. I'll give you some painkillers for today, but you should be back to normal by tomorrow."

"Your. . .hand?" I blurted out clumsily as he pulled away. It was definitely glowing, and I wasn't just seeing things. That or I was reeeaaalllyyyy out of it. Which I kinda was, not gonna lie.

"Oh!" He blinked at me for a second, eyes wide and hands flying back in shock. Then, he let out an embarrassed laugh, "It's normal, I promise. It's just my power; I can heal most injuries as long as I know the steps to recovery. Though. . .if something doesn't have a cure, there isn't much I can do. . .Anyway! I dubbed it Healing Touch! Cool, huh?"

"Um, yeah. . ." I said as I sat up. I meant to nod, but instantly a grimace overtook my face as a twinge of pain went from one ear to another. I raised my hand to try and rub soothing circles into my skull when, suddenly, a paper cup full of water gently tapped against my cheek. I moved my hand to see the man from before offering a set of pills along with the cup, "Here, this will help."

I took the water and pills gratefully. It was hard to gulp everything down, but by the time I was done, he had grabbed his swivel chair, dragged it to the side of my bed, and sat down on it backwards. His hands rested gently on the plush back, and his chin dug into the cushion when he tilted his head, "So, do you remember anything?"

"A dodgeball game from hell?" I said, but it came out more like a question as I handed him the paper cup. He hummed, grabbed it, then crumpled the cup in one hand and tossed it into the basin near his desk. It swished, and the mystery nurse-man let out a triumphant, "Made it! Take that, Ben!"

"Ben?"

He turned back to me with a shrug, "My husband. He says my aim is awful," His expression turned exasperated, and he let out a small puff of air, "Really, it's not like he's any better. He can't play basketball to save his life!"

I blinked, "Oh."

"Yeah," He said, waving his arm in a circle to prove his point, "I know, right. Total Hypocrite. Good thing I love him so much, the doof."

Knowing how people treated Alex's moms, I felt like I needed to say: "My best friend has two moms, and I love them both to death. Like, seriously, Bethany and Laura are the best!"

I couldn't help but feel like cringing the moment the words left my mouth. I just used the 'I have a friend that's gay sentiment that every straight person likes to use when something like this comes up.

Like, big oof, right?

He let out a soft sound, but then his eyes widened when he came to a sudden realization, "Oh! I never introduced myself, did I?"

"No, you didn't," I said. I couldn't tell if he was trying to change the subject or not but decided to just go with it just in case. Though, I wouldn't have minded if he talked more about Ben. The stories Oliver (oops, spoiler) has told me are soooo good. *Chef's kiss*

He stuck out his hand for me to shake, "My name is Oliver, and I'm Freedom Bay Highschool's full-time nurse. Nice to meet you, Skylar."

I took his hand, figuring that he probably knew my name from a file or something, "Nice to meet you too."

I let go, and my hand fell onto the thin mattress, "So, am I healthy, Doc?"

"Hmm, let's see. . ." He put his hand to his chin dramatically, his smile playful, "What else do you remember?"

"Ella hit me in the back of the head." I offered nonchalantly with a wave of my hand, a grin forming on my lips, "Like, Ow, right?"

"Indeed she did," He nodded his head in sympathy as if showing off a fair amount of untold wisdom—the dork. I could see why Ben liked him. "Turns out that girl has quite an arm."

"Well, she has super strength, so. . ."

"How many fingers?" He asked so abruptly and loudly that I jumped a little. My eyes locked on him, but his hands never left the chair and just smiled at me, waiting.

"Uhh. . .is this a trick question?" I asked with a raised eyebrow after a few seconds of him staring at me.

He let out a small laugh and shook his head, "Well, I think you'll be fine."

"So I pass?"

"Yes."

"Cool."

"Yup."

". . ."

". . ."

"So . . ." I said awkwardly after a very, very long minute of looking at the health-related posters plastered to the walls around us, "Can I go now?"

He let out another laugh, this one coming deep from his chest. He leaned back into his laughter, almost falling out of his swivel chair, "Sorry, sorry, I was just messing with you."

He pushed off with his feet and twirled until he was back at his desk. He stood up and rummaged around for a pen. He ripped a piece off what I thought was an important document and wrote down two phone numbers. "Yes, you can go. Here are my school and personal numbers. If the pain persists when you wake up tomorrow, come and see me, okay? Or give me a call. Either's fine."

"Okay," I acknowledged as I went to get up after taking the paper from him. And like an idiot, I got up too fast, resulting in a hiss of pain, "Ow. . . "

Oliver sighed, "The meds should kick in soon, but please take it easy. She did a number to your skull, and as much as I loved our conversion, I'd rather you not end up here *too* soon." I nodded slowly, and he squeezed my shoulder, "Now go on to the dorms; class is over for today."

That caught my attention, and I looked him dead in the eyes when I asked, "Wait, how long was I out?"

His face was as neutral as he could manage when he told me the bitter truth, "A little over a day. . . It's Around 9:30 at night. Monday. They brought you here a little after 7:00 yesterday."

"Oh." I said stupidly, and his willpower broke, a gentle but slightly amused smile lining his lips, "Yeah, sorry about that. Usually, healing doesn't take that long. I had to be careful not to mess up. Head injuries are tricky."

He winked, "But don't worry though, I'm sure that not too much happened while you were gone."

Oh, I wish that was the truth. Because that one day, one measly day, was when you decided to ruin my life. And sure, none of my classmates told me about the assignment. *And sure,* you could say you forgot to mention it to me, but we both know that's a. . .

Big.

Fat.

Lie.

The only plus side was that you gave me a free pass to every other assignment I missed that dreaded day in the infirmary. But was it worth it, though?

No.

No, it was not.

Hey, Teach, this is Micah.

I just want to point out that we didn't mean to _not_ tell him. It was more like everyone else kinda thought someone else did it. . . You know, like, miscommunication? So yeah. . . oops?

Also sorry Sky . . . : (

I'm not sure when he snagged this from me in the few days he was at my house, but apology not accepted.

*****

I stumbled into the dorms about thirty minutes after telling Oliver thank you (and doing the walk of shame back into the office to get my forgotten shoes, much to Oliver's amusement). It took me so long to get back because every time I thought that 'hey, maybe I could go faster without my head feeling like someone hit it with a super strength-infused dodgeball,' it would prove me wrong. Oliver told me almost offhandedly as I left (the second time) that the headache was more from his healing than the injury itself. Still a pain, though. Especially when some of the older kids wandering around would look at me like I was drunk.

I guess I kinda was? Healing drunk? Is that a thing?

I pushed through the main door of the dorms and I noticed that the piece Ella had accidentally destroyed was gone. Triston must have replaced it while I was out. I closed the door behind me and looked out to see a few people lounging on the couches and watching a rousing game of Smash Bros.

Micah, the ultimate assignment snatcher apparently, saw me first, tipping his head back at the sound of the door opening, "Oh, hey Skylar, looks like you are-"

"I'm so, so sorry!" Ella sprang up from the stool she was sitting on in the kitchen and trotted over to me, wringing her hands anxiously. She looked like she was about to cry, so I was quick to wave her off with a smile, "No, Hey, Ella, it's okay. I know you didn't mean to."

"Still, I feel awful about it. . ."

"Really, it's fine," I reassured, lightly putting my hand on her shoulder, "I'll just know to duck next time, yeah?"

Ella looked like she was about to apologize again, but before she could get anything out, a sharp cry came from the direction of the TV. We both jumped at the sound.

"Yes! Ahahahahaha!" Layla cheered as she threw her arms up in victory, the remote flying out of her hand and skidding to a stop at my feet.

That's why you wear the strap, Layla.

Haha, as if anyone wears the strap. What are we? Heathens?

"Gah, I can't believe I lost to a Miil A Miil" Jake yelled as his twin laughed so hard he fell off the arm of the couch and onto the floor, his legs comically sticking up so that you can see only his sneakers.

"Hey man," Warren said with a shit-eating grin from the armchair, crossing his legs, "You just suck. It's not the Mii's fault you have no talent."

"I had such high hopes for you too. . ." Jason said seriously with a shake of his head. His serious expression lasted for maybe one second before he broke and started laughing too.

"Alright, you are ALL the worst!"

As Jake argued that he totally didn't suck and he could beat Layla anytime (Layla snorted, which did not help de-escalate the situation at all), I bent down to pick up the long-forgotten remote. I instantly regretted it as pain shot through my temple, and I almost dropped the remote as it slipped slightly in my hand. I let out a groan and rubbed my head when I was fully standing upright.

"You okay, dude?" Micah asked, his hands outstretched in a sign of concern. You know, the standard 'I don't know how to help, so I'm gonna stick out my hands as if that will solve anything' gesture. I didn't even see him get off the couch; maybe I was more out of it than I thought.

I handed him the remote and rubbed my eyes, "I'm fine, but. . .I think I'm gonna call it a night."

Micah let out a sympathetic sigh, "Okay, feel better."

"Do you need anything?" Ella asked, the worry palpable in the air around her.

"No, no, I'm fine." I smiled, "I just want to sleep so I can go to class tomorrow."

"Fair warning," Micah said as he waved me off, "Mr. Nightlight is already up there."

"Ugh," I complained as I waited for the elevator, "Maybe he'll be asleep?"

Micah shrugged, and the elevator doors snapped shut before either of us could reply.

As it turned out, Nolan was sitting at his desk when I walked into our shared room. He glanced my way when I flopped onto my bed without taking off my shoes. I laid there in silence, my face buried in my blankets, until I heard the sound of Nolan's office chair moving, the wheels scuffing against the hardwood.

I tilted my head to look towards him and saw that he had turned himself around to face me.

I raised an eyebrow at him after a few seconds, "What?"

His lip twitched, and he hesitated for a second until he let out a sigh, the sound long and deep, "Fuck, it's nothing. Just–"

With a growl, he turned sideways towards his desk and grabbed a stack of papers. He threw it at me full force with a grunt, and I barely dodged, the packet landing only inches from my nose. I glared at him as I sat up, "What the hell, dude!"

Nolan already had his back turn to me, focused back on what he was doing at his desk. His shoulders seemed to collapse inwards, "Just read it. You're lucky I even agreed to give it to you in the first place."

"Wow, *thank you so much*." I let out sarcastically, but the only reaction I got was a slight burst of red flaring out of Nolan's brown curls. Deciding that it wasn't worth my time to deal with my annoying roommate (and my head was still killing me too, that jerk), I averted my eyes to the packet I had so rudely received. It was about five to six pages and had words printed on both sides. It seemed to be a cheat sheet for what I missed while I was in the infirmary.

Fun.

I flipped through pages lazily until I read the words in large bold letters on the front:

Must have your <u>ALIAS</u> picked out by the end of Vigilante Studies <u>tomorrow.</u> (Other than that, I don't care if you finish anything else. Less for me to grade.)

. . .I feel like. . .maybe not reading this packet was my downfall. . .BUT your note didn't help, okay! Talk about mixed messages!

"Well, at least he's honest," I breathed out. I tossed the packet onto my nightstand and rolled over in bed, nuzzling my face into my pillow. I closed my eyes. . .

Then they snapped open, my body jolting upright as I yelled out, "Wait! Vigilante names already! Ah, crap! I'm so screwed!"

Nolan let out a long, deep, and suffering sigh: "You're an idiot."

☁ Chapter 8 ☁

    I didn't go to sleep until really late that night, much to Nolan's annoyance. I sat at my desk, only lit up by the flashlight on my slowly dying phone, and contemplated what I wanted my Alias to be. (Only after Nolan threw something at my head for the third time did I cave and switch off the room's lights. Childish revenge, I know, but I felt validated after the infamous nightlight incident).

    There were so many options for my Vigilante name: Funny, clever, intimating, intense, a pun, a combination of all of those, but I never found one I was satisfied with. I ended up conking out at my desk at three in the morning, my pencil falling to the floor from my loosened grip and a small puddle of drool coating my notes.

    SLAM!

I woke up with a start, almost falling out of my chair. I scrambled to figure out what the loud noise was, the paper floating to the floor with my aggressive spasms. I spun in a panic until I spotted Nolan lying on the hardwood floor next to me, cursing and still in his pajamas. He growled and grabbed the pencil I had dropped the night before and hurled it angrily across the dorm. It bounced off the wall and landed innocently on Nolan's bed.

Silence, then:

"Ohhhhh, you slipped on my pencil..." I said in a slow, sleepy realization. Which in hindsight probably wasn't the right thing to say but, ya know, too late now. I tried not to look at him as Nolan glared at me and grit his teeth, his hands clenching and unclenching until he let out a loud and aggravated, "Fuckin-"

I avoided his eyes because I honestly felt like, Oops, that was my bad, but I didn't want to say it to his face. Instead, my gaze wandered above his head and towards my bed. . .

"Holy crap!" I yelled, cutting Nolan off from his rant (which, honestly, I kinda deserved. The rant, not cutting him off). I had looked at the digital clock on my nightstand to find that I only had twenty minutes to get dressed, run across campus, and slide into my seat before I was late to class. I scrambled to grab my phone, to see that maybe I was just losing my mind, and it wasn't the time I thought it was, but my phone was dead. I flung myself out of my chair and towards my closet, "Gah, It's so late! Why didn't you wake me up!"

Nolan looked like he was about ready to smack me upside the head. He quickly got onto his feet, "It's because of you that I slept through my alarm! And, you utter dumbass, that's what I was *doing!*"

I paused, a pair of pants dangling from my hands, "Wait, seriously?"

Like, wow, right? Who would have thought that Nolan, of all people, would have the decency to help another human being? *gasp* I gotta say that I was shocked. Nolan made a face as he pulled on a pair of pants with way more force than necessary, the intense glare piercing through me.

You would think that the silence would be horrifying and that I would take the hint and not do something arguably stupid, but my brain decided that that was the perfect time to tease him. I smiled at him sweetly as my head popped out of my shirt, "Oh, so you *do* care about people! Cute."

Nolan's eyes flared a terrifying, fiery red. He lunged, his arms outstretched to strangle me. I dodged and grabbed my backpack that was next to my bed, hurriedly shoving stuff inside as Nolan tried to kill me. After acquiring everything and slipping on only one shoe and stuffing the other one in my bag for safekeeping, I flung myself out the door.

"You better put on a shirt! Don't want to get expelled on your second day!" I yelled.

Nolan slid out the door, very much without his shirt, and chased me down the hall. In a last-ditch effort to grab me before I made it to either the stairs or the elevator, he jumped, sending us both to the floor with a crash, my backpack flying helplessly away. We struggled there for a long moment, the tussle intense and not one-sided.

There was the sound of a door opening next to us, and Ethan calmly walked out. He blinked at us from above and stepped around our flailing bodies to get to the elevator. He turned to us, opened his mouth, closed it, and stepped through the doors when they slid open with a '*ding!*'.

"Hey, you're just gonna let him kill me?" I asked, half-joking and half-seriously as I struggled under Nolan; my hand reached out for help. But Ethan just saluted me, his face showing his thought process of 'Not gonna get involved with *that*,' and let the doors close.

My jaw dropped, and my hand fell to the floor in defeat.

Way to leave a bro hanging!

"'I'll remember that!" I yelled even though Ethan probably couldn't hear me anymore. My words oozed the utter betrayal that I felt, "See if I help you when you're getting murdered!"

Then something unbelievable happened.

A miracle.

A once in a lifetime occurrence. . .

Nolan *snorted.*

Like, a full-on pig snort of a laugh. So loud that it *echoed* around the hall. I froze, he froze, and the shocked silence between us was mutual. I pulled an Ethan and opened and closed my mouth like a fish as Nolan was like a statue above me.

"Uh. . .let's make a deal," I said slowly, as if I was trying not to startle a small animal, "I won't tell people you snort like a pig when you laugh, and you won't kill me right now. . .Deal?"

It was almost instantaneous as he unfroze and got up from the floor, his back ramrod straight. He stared at me for a moment before walking back to our dorm, leaving me lying on the floor, "Deal. This will go to your grave, *got it?*"

"Yep!" I squeaked in a regretfully unmanly way. The only answer I got was a harsh and loud slamming of our door.

I got the heck out of there before he could change his mind.

*****

"Dude, you look like you just came out of a hurricane," Jason said as I hurried into the classroom and took the seat beside him. I dumped my bag on the floor and slumped into my chair, out of breath.

"Are you sure you're okay to come to class?" Will said worriedly from behind me, eyeing my disheveled hair and clothes warily.

I tried to explain through my heavy breathing, "Late. Ran. Tried to fly, realized. . . .that I can't fly 'cause . . .secret. Ate shit. Nolan's scary. Ethan didn't save me."

Jason and Will shared a look, and I was too out of breath and sleep-deprived to care that they probably thought I still had a concussion.

"Can confirm. I did not save him." Ethan, the traitor, decided that NOW was the time to come to my aid with a shrug, not that I totally couldn't have used that earlier but whatever.

"Ah, well," Will said as he fiddled with the turtle hair clip holding back his bangs, "At least. . .you made it on time?"

I nodded, and at that moment, the door slammed open, and Nolan stumbled in, his hair equally messy and wild as my own. The bell rang only a few seconds later. Saved by the bell.

Wait, that's not the correct expression, is it?

Just in the nick of time.

There we go.

"Huh," Harley said innocently as he watched Nolan with eager eyes, "I didn't know you took school so seriously, Nolan! I'm impressed by the dedication!"

"Shut. Up. Kid." Nolan barely got out before he collapsed into his chair and slammed his head down on his desk with a *thunk!*. Micah winced at the sound from the seat next to him.

"Um, do I want to know the whole story?" Jason asked in a stage whisper.

"Probably not," I said honestly, slumping further into my chair.

"Ok, well, uh. Glad to have you in class?" Jason said in a very obvious attempt at changing the subject.

What a pure dude.

I let out a small snort, and once I could breathe normally again, I said sincerely, a smile on my face, "You know what? Me too."

Jason smiled back.

After that, the day was relatively normal. I learned some things, watched the morning announcements, and ate a freakin' good lunch in the cafeteria. (Like, did all the budget for the school go into lunch? Oh, wait, it went to the slide, lol). I found out that everyone had the same schedule as me except for our electives, which were the last two classes of the day. I also found out that you were our only teacher except for electives. Which was weird for two reasons: 1. I found out that you're stinkin' smart (don't let that get to your over-inflated head), and 2. I had gone all through middle school with people telling me I would have to move to different classes and that that would be the new norm.

But really, was anything about my time at this school normal?

No.

It wasn't.

So, moving on.

After classes were over, everyone had a few hours before he had to make the trek to Vigilante Studies. Some people bemoaned the thought of having to hike the Trail of Doom, or whatever it was called, while others tried to enjoy their freedom while it lasted (or not, some did homework instead, goodyto-shoes). I dropped off my bag upstairs and sat down on the couch next to Micah, resting my eyes.

Why did I stay up so late again?

Oh, that's right.

I didn't bother opening my eyes when I asked, "So, did you come up with a name yet?"

I couldn't see, but I assumed that Micah nodded, "Mmhmm. Though I'm not sure if I like it all that much."

I opened one eye to gauge his expression, "At least you came up with one. I got nothing."

Micah hummed again and sat back more on the couch, his gaze moving towards the ceiling in thought, "Sky Skimmer?"

"Mmm, I'm not feeling that. Thanks, though."

"Tornado Man?"

I shook my head and sat up slightly, "I don't think I could control the weather. . .wait, could I?"

Micah seemed to consider that for a moment, ". . .Maybe? Like you could fly really fast in a circle or something and cause a dust devil?"

I titled my head as I contemplated that suggestion, "That seems more like a Layla thing. . ."

"Yeah. . . Skywalker?"

"I think we would have legal trouble with that one."

"Okay, I could see that. . .Hmm, how 'bout Jet stream?"

The conversation continued like that for a long time. But, eventually, Micah and I gave up on thinking of a name, and I just hoped I could come up with one before I got to class. We ended up playing games for about an hour and got a snack from the cafeteria. Then we met up with everyone to sneak behind our dorm, and I noted that mostly everyone was dressed for a long, long hike. Adaptation at its finest right there.

The walk wasn't as eventful as the first time. Our bodies somewhat adjusted to the change they had undergone to give us powers. There were a few slip-ups, though. Ethan still got attacked by trees, but it was less frequent (and aggressive). Layla was long gone from the first step she took, bolting up the trail with a yelp and disappearing to never be seen again. And Kalei's hand had caught fire, almost sending Ella's braid ablaze.

Honestly, I was thinking at the time that we were doing a pretty good job at keeping the powers thing a secret. Who would have thunk? Maybe we could make it the whole year and beyond without outing ourselves as vigilantes. . .

Anyway, when we got to the end of the hike, we found you sitting at a picnic bench amidst many more benches, scrolling through your phone. Once you spotted us, you tucked your phone away and stood up, "Alright, you're all here."

"What about Layla?" Harley asked with a raised hand.

"Over there." You said as you pointed to a seemingly passed-out Layla lying on the grass about a hundred feet away. Hearing her name, she turned, so she was on her side facing us, her breathing hard and fast, "Hi. . .just stopped. . .running. . ."

"You good?" Jason yelled to her, and she raised a shaky thumbs-up, her smile a little wobbly.

"She'll be fine." You waved off our concern and then gestured to the benches around you, "Take a seat. I don't care where but make sure to grab a whiteboard and pen."

We grabbed the items and got settled, Jason making a detour to help Layla up and bring her to one of the benches, which she gave him a thankful smile for. Once everyone was comfortable, you went to the front and put your hands in your pockets, "Okay, you got another ten minutes to think of your Alias'. . . be grateful I'm so nice. After that, you'll be presenting them, and when everyone's done, we can go back; I don't want to be here forever. I'm tired."

"Wait, let me get this straight," Jake asked, "You made us take the Walk of Doom to just do a few presentations, that's it?"

"Uh-huh." You said, looking at Jake, unimpressed, "Unless you want me to make you run the obstacle course again today."

Jake backpedaled wisely, "Nah, I'm good. Thanks for being so merciful today."

"Obstacle course?" I asked Warren, who was looking at Jake like he thought he was an idiot. You know, I'm noticing now that Warren and the twins have a weird love-hate friendship going on. Not my business though, they can work it out themselves.

Shaking his head, Warren turned towards me and pointed at something in the distance. I had to squint to make it out, "The obstacle course was what we did yesterday. It was hell."

"Yeah, and Ethan got stuck upside down for sooo long, it was really funny," Harley said with mirth in his eyes, oblivious to Ethan's scowl from behind him.

Micah stage whispered beside me, "His plants wrapped around his legs. It took him like ten minutes for him to convince them to stop."

Oh, gosh, I am so sorry, Ethan.

Even though you didn't help out a Bro back when I was almost killed, I still wouldn't wish that on anybody.

"That had to have *sucked*," I replied in sympathy.

Micah and Warren both nodded and let out a synchronized, "Mmmhmm."

"You have eight minutes." You said from where you sat on the ground, your back leaning against the building. You also looked smug when we started writing frantically on our whiteboards in a mad scramble of squeaking markers: did I mention how much I hate you?

What happened next was seven and a half minutes of pure writer's block agony. (About 30 seconds of it was me realizing that I never found out who won the Dodgeball Game from Hell and what the reward was. Yes, I know I get distracted easily; sue me, I was curious. Apparently, my team had won in the end despite my head injury, and you took them to McDonald's. So. . .you owe me a Big Mac.) As the time ticked down, I still couldn't think of anything, erasing what I wrote on my whiteboard and rewriting something else instead. At the very last second, I wrote down the only thing I could think of that I was at least a little bit satisfied with and hoped I didn't sound like a total fool when I went up to present.

137

There was a chirp of your alarm going off, and you stood up, "Times up. Who wants to go first? Come on up, don't be shy. The faster we get this over with, the faster I can get out of here."

After a significant pause, you sighed long and hard, "Alright, I'll just choose then. Jake, since you think I'm *so very merciful*, why don't you go first."

Chase snorted at his brother's betrayed face, "Fail."

"Oh, shut up." Jake snarked and hit his twin with his whiteboard, satisfied with the squeak that came out of his brother. He strode the front, "Alright, now or never!"

He flipped his board around and shoved it towards us excitedly, "My Alias is: Body Double! You know, because I can make clones."

"You didn't need to explain it," Warren said, exasperated as everyone politely clapped.

You looked somewhat impressed as you said, "Not bad. It's easy to say and represents your power well. Good job."

Jake looked shocked at the praise, but he wasn't gonna correct you. A compliment from you is like getting full marks on a test that was impossible to ace in the first place.

You just take the win and move on while you still can.

Ryuma got up next, and my only thought was that he probably wanted to get this over with, which is a sound strategy for doing presentations. It's best to go as one of the first ones, and then people forget about it by the time everyone else has gone.

Foolproof when your presentation sucks.

Jake gave Ryuma's shoulder a reassuring squeeze before he left to sit back down. How nice of him, though part of me suspected that Ryu would have a permanent handprint on his clothes. (It's happened before.) Everyone waited as Ryuma seemed to get his courage, and he timidly spun his board around. On it was the Kanji: 幽霊, pronounced as Yuurei.

Thanks, Ryu, for showing me how to write that.

"Yuurei. . .It means ghost, uh, the western kind. . ." Ryuma said to the polite, yet a little bit confused, applause he received. It was mainly because we didn't know how to read kanji, but the clapping got louder when we actually knew what it meant.

"Yoshida, that's a cool name!" Layla shouted in encouragement as Ryuma nodded shyly and made his way back to his seat.

"Yeah, it's super clever," Jason said with a reassuring smile. Ryu looked a little like he wanted to sink into the ground, and not a second after I thought that, his legs went transparent. Jason let out a gasp but quickly pulled him back up and onto the bench, holding him in place until he became solid again.

After a long while of not-so-awkward silence, Warren sighed in defeat and got up, "Guess I'm next then."

Warren weaved his way to stand where everyone could see him and, with another sigh, flipped his board around. He got straight to the point, "Compact Burst. That's my alias."

Everyone clapped, but it was slow and not very loud. It had more to do with having a small cluster of people than not liking the name, but Warren felt the need to say more anyway, "Because I can Compact myself. . .And burst upward. . . .I thought it was a good name, okay!?"

Warren glared at Chase, who was smirking at him. His brother not far behind as he started to snicker, "You don't need to *explain*, Warren."

Warren's eye twitched a little as his own words were thrown back in his face. He threw his whiteboard down hard and shouted, "Shut up! Get your ass up here if you have a better name, you idiot!"

Chase looked like he achieved a great victory, "Gladly, your highness. I would be honored to share such a wondrous name with you."

Warren threw his maker at Chase's head, but Chase went invisible and appeared a few feet away from where the pen landed, "Missed me~."

Warren sat down roughly and clenched his fist as Chase took his place to present. I faintly heard Warren say under his breath, "I know where you sleep."

Well, that's not worrying or anything. I placed a hand on his shoulder before patting it lightly. Surprisingly he didn't smack my hand away.

Chase cleared his throat dramatically, "Alright! What Yall been waiting for ("Did he just say 'Yall'?")... I am the vigilante... Trickster!"

Warren threw his hands in the air, "How was that better than my name!?"

Chase's mouth opened to explain exactly why his name was so much better when his head was roughly shoved to the side by Adya, "Move it, loser. I'm next."

"I didn't even see her get up," Micah stuttered, and I nodded in amazement as I watched her glare at Chase. He raised his hands and slowly backed away, "Okay, just don't stab me."

Hmm, someone seems traumatized.

Noted.

She scowled at him, Chase smiled nervously, and Jason whispered out in a sigh, "Why'd you give her the idea, dude?"

Jason's question was never answered. Instead, Adya straightened up proudly and proclaimed, "I'm Manifest."

And that was it. She just sat down as if nothing had happened. It was a different kind of intimidation. Like, who would want to go after that?

Harley, apparently.

He must've not sensed the weird tension in the air because he skipped up to the front, his smile large and inviting, "So! I wanted to say that Layla helped me pick mine out. Thank you again, Layla!" He held out his board with an even bigger smile, "I am the vigilante: SweetTalk! Because I'm sweet and can talk to animals!"

"Yes, you are, hun!" Layla yelled from the back, her face taking on a proud older sister's look. Harley beamed, and I couldn't help but clap a little louder.

Honestly, that kid deserves to be happy.

I'd kill a man for him.

Harley took in the applause and bowed like he just finished off an amazing performance of a play. Then, he turned to Layla and lifted his arms to gesture towards her, "The floor is yours!"

Layla put a hand to her chest and got up with a flourish. She cleared her throat with a nod and said dramatically, "Yes! Thank you, Harley!"

Harley gave her a thumbs-up as they switched places, and that only made Layla more ecstatic as she continued, "I'm the vigilante Shooting Star! Because I'm fast, and I'm going to be a star, haha! Cute, huh?"

Everyone clapped, and Layla marched over to Ella and grabbed her arm, "Come on, I know yours is just as cute. You can do this!"

Ella blushed and hid her face in her hands. That didn't stop Layla from pulling her to the front and leaving her with a: 'You got this!'. Ella swallowed and gripped the edges of her broad, a crack appearing on the edges. She bit her lip and slowly, timidly, spun her board around, "Um. . . My name. . . . is Elegance."

Warren, who now that I look back on it, had it really, *really* bad for Ella, yelled, "That's a great name. It suits you!"

"Yep!" Layla said as she leaned heavily on her hand, her body language proud, "She goes around with grace and elegance until you get on her bad side! Haha! Whack, slap, and you're down! It's perfect!"

Ella shielded her face with her whiteboard, her cheeks doing an outstanding job at imitating a tomato, and sat back down, "Layla, stop."

"Nah, girl, you need the praise."

Will decided to have mercy on the poor girl and distract everyone from her ever-growing embarrassment. Fiddling with the clip in his hair, he awkwardly got himself ready to present, "It's not very original but. . .my vigilante name is Deep Dive."

"Oh," You perked up at the name, "Like that vigilante from a hundred years ago? The one that can feel people's emotions?"

Will nodded and smiled, "Yeah. Even though he didn't have the same power as me, he did amazing things and helped a lot of people figure themselves out. . .helped them from turning down the wrong path. . . .it just felt right, I guess."

You tilted your head in thought, "I hope you're ready to be able to live up to a name like that."

Will seemed to deflate a bit, but then his gaze became firm, his shoulders determined, "Yes, I am."

"Wow," Micah said beside me.

You shrugged, "Well, good luck then."

Will gave you an affirmative nod, and I couldn't help looking at what I wrote down. It didn't have any sort of meaning, and it wasn't even that good of a name. Using my sleeve, I erased and wrote something else down. Even though I still wasn't quite satisfied, I felt like I could give this one a more significant meaning if I tried enough. And it was a pun, so that was a bonus.

I was so lost in thought I didn't even realize that Jason had volunteered to go next. I barely got back to the introduction in time to find out what his name was: SteadFast.

Jason laughed awkwardly and rubbed the back of his neck, "You know. . . like I will be an immovable force? And strong?"

"And because you stick to things?" Chase finished for him.

Jason made a face but nodded with a sigh, ". . . Yes. Because I can stick to things."

"Way to steal his thunder, bro," Jake almost sounded like he was scolding his twin, which just couldn't be possible. There was just no way. But. . .stranger things have happened so. . . ‾_(ツ)_/‾

"Well, I think it's a perfect name," I said matter of factly as Jason sat down next to me. He gave me a look between being thankful and trying to see if I was messing with him. Like, how rude Jason. Can't a friend support another friend? Geez.

Speaking of friends, it was now Micah's awaited turn to present. I thought about our previous conversion, which only made me more curious about what he came up with. He still didn't seem very confident, but he didn't let his voice show it as he said, "The name I chose is Shifted. . . because I can shapeshift."

You nodded, and Micah let out a sigh of relief, "Good job."

When Micah came back, I elbowed him, "What were you worrying about? That name's good."

Micah struggled to find an answer for a second but ended up shrugging, "I don't know? It just seemed kinda lame in my head."

"Eh, it's fine. I've heard a lot worse names. Just wait for mine."

Micah raised an eyebrow and leaned over to read what I wrote, but I quickly covered it up, "No Spoilers!"

Micah laughed, "Okay, fine. Though I bet it's not all that bad."

I shrugged, "Only time will tell."

"You're a dork, you know that?"

"Thanks!"

"Guys, Kalei's trying to go," Jason whispered to us, a little panicked. I looked up to see Kalei giving me a stern stare from the front, her hand on fire, looking like she was about ready to throw it. I got flashbacks from the Dodgeball Game from Hell, and all I could get out was, "Oh, oops?"

She rolled her eyes and shook her hand to dispel the flames, and I couldn't help but feel like I got off easy for some reason. At that moment, I mentally jotted down not to mess with her. Adya might be scary, but Kalei was a different kind of terrifying. Like, sure, Adya could stab me if she wanted, but Kalei could burn me alive.

I'd take a stabbing any day, thank you.

Kalei pushed her bangs out of her face, and her eyes were a determined kinda fire as she stated, "I went with the name Heat Edge. I did think about other names like Inferno and Combustion, but I wanted it to be a little gentler but intimidating. To show that you shouldn't mess with me but that I will always be there to help you whenever I can. At least that was my thought process anyway."

You hummed, "It's good to think about that stuff when coming up with a name. Because at the end of the day, you're there to help people."

Kalei nodded and seemed to take to heart what you said. It was one of your 'Okay, sometimes you can be cool and knowledgeable' moments. And

I'll admit that you do have those moments a lot, but I don't have to like it.

I was planning on going next when you spoke up, standing and popping your back loudly, "Okay, we have three more. No more lollygagging. Ethan, you're next, then Nolan and Skylar. Let's get this over with. I have things to do."

"But I thought you were tired?" Harley asked innocently but was ignored.

Ethan, on the other hand, looked like he wanted to gut you. It seemed like he did NOT want to go next. That's totally the reason you chose him, wasn't it? And going by the look on your face, I could tell my guess was right, "Come on up, Ethan, we don't have all night."

As Ethan walked up reluctantly and slightly angry, I sat back and thought that I would just have to wait. Going now or waiting for a couple more people didn't matter anyway. Whatever. Though, I did kinda want to go next. I was building up my courage, a whole speech waiting in the back of my head, but that speech had long left, blowing away in the wind.

Was that ALSO why you said for the other two to go first?

Evil, pure evil.

Ethan looked a little bit like he wanted to die, "Fine! Reluctantly. . . .I went with the name Cultivate because it was the best option for my stupid power. If you touch me one more time, I'm burning this *whole place to the ground.*"

The bush behind him abruptly shifted back where it was initially as if it was a kid caught stealing cookies, and Ethan just looked so tired. I wouldn't be surprised if he asked Kalei to be an accomplice to his plan.

The man was having a hard few days.

. . .I guess I could give him a break about not saving me from Nolan. Just this once, he can have a free pass.

Anyway, moving on, next came Nolan, who looked like he just wanted to hit something. Even though he glared at everyone, I couldn't take it seriously; once you hear The Snort, you can never go back. Nolan let out another one of his long and suffering sighs, "My vigilante name is Blindsided. Happy?"

You just smiled, and Nolan let out a huff and went back to his seat. It was now or never. I got up, leaving my whiteboard behind. The speech that I was slowly planning throughout the presentations was now completely gone. I don't get stage fright, but for some reason, I froze up. Maybe it was the importance of that moment. Whatever I said next would be with me for a long, long time. And in the end, I decided to do what I always do best.

I winged it.

"My name is SkyRocket! Evildoers will fear me, people will feel safe, and with me as a vigilante, I'll make sure that peace will, uh, skyrocket! That's my promise to the world!"

I ended my dramatic reveal with a pose of pure victory and waited for the applause that I deserved; thank you.

"Pfft, hahaha, Skylar!" Micah choked out a laugh as he clapped, "It was so worth the wait, hahaha."

Nolan slammed his head against the table, *"Why?"*

I wasn't fazed, though, by anyone's comments. Sure, my performance was a total cringe-fest, and my name could have been way cooler, but It felt right. Because no matter what happened, I felt like I was going to skyrocket to the top. Be the best vigilante I could be.

Plus, it didn't hurt that my name was kinda, sorta, a pun.

That's the best part, honestly.

☁ Chapter 9 ☁

It wasn't until a whole week later that we got to do a meaningful vigilante exercise. (Also, I got my contacts, so now I could finally see things without having to squint. Nice!). The days before that were filled with us walking to the training grounds after our regular classes only for us to turn back because you had a date (Wed.), your date stood you up, and now you had to wallow in ice cream (Thurs.), making us wait a whole hour only to message us on the class group chat that you 'can't make it, sorry' (Fri.), and eventually telling us that those were all lies and that you were just letting us get used to 'walking up a mountain every day, now go do the obstacle course' (Mon.).

By the way, we all knew the date part wasn't a lie.

"So, do you think we'll have to run the obstacle course again?" Micah asked as we rounded the last bend before we got to the end of the trail.

I shrugged, and Warren scoffed from behind us. He marched forward, his shoulders tensing up a bit in his red tracksuit jacket, "Who knows with our idiot of a teacher."

Layla turned around and started walking backward from the front of the group, her ponytail bouncing with each step, "Hey, if my date stood me up, I would be sad too."

Warren made a face and shoved his hands into his shorts pockets, "He's a grown-ass adult. That's not an excuse."

Layla tilted her head, and her smile turned a little vicious, "So, say if a pretty girl with long brown hair that had, I don't know, *super strength* stood you up, you wouldn't be sad?"

Warren's face resembled the color of his jacket, "T-that- I'm . . . .not- Shut up!"

Layla's expression turned a little guilty but not guilty enough to not say, "Sorry, that was a low blow."

Warren glared at her as she turned around, and Micah and I shared a look because both of us were wondering the same thing: Did she mean to insult his height on purpose or. . . ?

Will threw an arm over Warren's shoulder, maybe to placate him, maybe not, "But that doesn't explain what happened on Friday, though."

Layla paused, "Eh, you got me there."

"Looks like something's going to happen today. Look," Jason said as he pointed to the far side of the clearing, near the building with the picnic benches. You were leaning against the wall, but you weren't alone. Triston was there with you, amicably talking while holding something small in his hands. You both seemed to be in a deep conversation, not noticing that we arrived yet.

"Is that a box the principal is holding?" Ryuma asked, and I almost jumped out of my skin and ascended to space out of fright. He was so quiet that I forgot he was there. I wasn't the only one as everyone else either jumped or outright gasped. Yes, even Adya. Though if she knew I just wrote that, she would kick me in the gut. You know me, always living dangerously. A certain someone would probably say that's my most annoying trait, but they aren't here to smack me right now, so, HA.

"Ah, C'mon Yoshida, I was about to scare them!" Chase pouted as he popped into existence beside us. His arms were crossed, and he honestly looked a little upset. Jake patted his shoulder ruefully, "You'll get them next time. . .now pay up. Hand over that twenty."

Ryuma smiled sheepishly as Chase scowled at his brother and handed over the money, "Ugh, whatever."

Triston perked up when he finally saw us. Holding the small cardboard box to his chest, he raised his other arm and waved us over, "Oh, Welcome! Come, come, gather around. We got something exciting for you guys today!"

"I hope it's not another slide," Nolan grumbled, and I couldn't help but snicker. I knew he didn't mean it to be funny, but just how he said it made me laugh. Nolan glared at me, and I retaliated by pushing up my nose to look like a pig's snout. Nolan gritted his teeth into a sneer and turned away, and I figured I won our battle of wills.

Triston laughed, "You think we have the budget for a second slide? Regrettably, it's just not in the cards, I'm afraid."

"That's not-. You know what? Forget it." Nolan said with the air of a man that has entirely given up on life.

Sad to see it, really.

He was so young.

Triston laughed good naturally and waved everyone closer, "Really, I'm sure you're going to find this interesting. Better than running that obstacle course, anyway."

You huffed indignantly, "Hey, the obstacle course is a great teaching method. Maybe next week I'll turn up the difficulty."

Everyone was startled a little bit. What the hell did *that* mean? The obstacle course was something you would see in military training, or maybe the police academy (and was just all-around awful to run through). How could he 'turn up the difficulty' when it was just an ordinary obstacle course? I glanced over at said course, and some of the ropes moved in the wind ominously.

"Oh, stop freaking them out, geez," Triston sighed with a shake of his head, "You make it sound so. . . *ominous.*"

"So, wait, he *can* turn up the difficulty?" Jason asked what we were all thinking.

"I wouldn't worry about it," Triston waved him off, which totally made us worry about it, "Anyway, it's time for some fun stuff!"

Harley bounced from one foot to the other, his hands behind his back as if he was trying to hold in some of his excitement with little success, "What is it?"

"Well, first off, Will, I have a present for you," Triston held up the box he was holding, and Will took it gingerly, "These are the clips we ordered for you. I hope you like them!"

Will let out a soft 'oh' and started to open the box as Triston continued with a clap of his hands, "Okay, question. What do you guys think is the most important thing a starting vigilante can learn?"

"How to kick someone's ass?" Adya offered with a smirk, crossing her arms.

Triston took in her sarcasm with grace and held up a finger, "That's part of it, sure, but how, pray tell, do you get good at kicking one's ass?"

"Learn martial arts?" Kalei suggested, straight-faced and serious.

"That too can be very helpful, but that's not until a little later. Firstly, what have you guys been having trouble with? That could cause a major issue if not addressed?"

There was a long silence before Will held up one of his new hair clips. This one was shaped like a sun, "For me, it would be that I can't choose when I read people's minds, and it physically hurts. . ."

"Precisely! Good job, Will!" Triston praised with such enthusiasm that Will blushed, "The first thing anyone starting out should learn is how to control their newfound powers. And why should we do this. . . Jake, you're up!"

"Uh," Jake jumped along with his clone beside him. . . when did he make that? "So we can get good at it?"

You let out a sigh and pushed yourself fully off the wall you were leaning on, "You have to learn control because of three major reasons," You held up a finger, adding more as you talked, "One: To make sure you do not accidentally use your powers without wanting it to happen. This can mean using it when you don't have your disguise or accidentally using your power against an innocent person."

You let that sink in before you continued, "Two: you will be able to enhance your powers to make them stronger. The more control you have will help you figure out your limitations and how to overcome them. And Three: to find out exactly what your powers can and cannot do. Sometimes people will go in thinking that their power is one thing, but it turns out it was something completely different the whole time."

Triston deflated a little, "Connor, you got to make them think a little for themselves."

You shrugged, and Triston just sighed, "Connor is right, though. We will work on control, limitations, and power progression for the next few months. By winter break, you guys will have a better understanding of what your powers can do and how to make them stronger."

We glanced at each other, and an excited chatter rang throughout the group. The overall consensus, from what I could tell, was: This is going to be fun.

Triston let us gush before he put his hands up in a placating gesture, "Ah, sorry to interrupt, but before you guys get too gung-ho, we have to go over the basics first."

Jake and Chase (and the clone) all groaned at the same time, "Ugh. We're about to get lectured, aren't we?"

Triston's smile was a little guilty. He held up his thumb and pointer finger apart, leaving a small gap, and winced, "Don't worry, it's only a *little* lecture, promise! You won't be quizzed on this or anything."

"Ahh, maybe you won't. . ." You said sadistically from behind Triston, and Triston was quick as he slapped your arm, "No, you will not!"

"Fine. . ."

"You'll have plenty of time to torture your students later, Connor." Triston sighed, "Now put on your big boy teacher pants and teach them something."

"Um, maybe we shouldn't encourage torture. . ." Micah spoke up, and I nodded my head quickly in agreement, "Yeah, not being tortured would be nice."

Triston lurched and waved his hands around aggressively, his eyes looking a bit panicked, "It was just a joke, a joke! We don't torture students!"

"Honestly, him panicking like that makes me think that it's the opposite. . ." Warren smiled as he joined in on the teasing.

"Mmmhmm." Jason nodded, trying not to laugh, "Fishy."

Triston frantically said, "Anyways-I"

"Changing the subject is also suspicious," Jake pointed out helpfully, while Chase cackled beside him, "Just to let you know. . ."

"Connor, you're already rubbing off on them!" Triston abandoned his diversion and turned to you with an exasperated expression.

You shrugged and said, "I'm so proud?"

"Wait, is he proud?" Ryuma asked innocently.

"Alright, alright, you gremlins! Sit down," Triston huffed, and maybe you *were* proud that we slowly broke your friend. The smile you had on your face said that you at least found it amusing. Either way, we collectively decided to take pity on Triston and sat down.

We're not entirely evil, after all.

Triston pointedly took a seat with us and tilted his head to the side as if to say, 'so are you wearing those big boy teaching pants?'.

You pouted a bit but started the lecture with a sigh, "There are different approaches to controlling powers. To pick the right one depends on where you fall in a 'power category.' You're either voluntary, involuntary, and semi-voluntary."

Harley's hand was in danger of flying off his wrist with how fast he swung it, "I have a question!"

You looked like you didn't want to acknowledge the interruption but decided to get it over with, "Yes, Harley?"

Harley lets out his question in a rush, "I get that powers can be voluntary and involuntary, but how can power be both? I know that mine is involuntary, based on how you categorized them. Since I'm always able to talk to animals, it would be involuntary. Also, by that logic, most everyone here has powers to turn off and on, so they are voluntary. Does Semi mean that part of your power you can turn off and on but the other part is subconscious or, like, duplicity? Like a part of your power can be used as a lie or deception? I've never heard of a power that can do both, so if it exists, it would probably be really rare. . .why are you looking at me like that?"

Halfway through Harley's little speech, your mouth had slowly fallen agape along with most everyone else. Triston took one look at our expressions and laughed, almost choking on his own spit by how hard he cracked up, "Did he, haha, not tell you? Also, Connor, why are you so surprised you read his file!"

Harley blushed a deep scarlet and fidgeted in his seat, "Sorry, I was mumbling again, wasn't I?"

"Kid stole my thunder," You let out, and Harley looked even more embarrassed. Triston just beamed and put a comforting hand on Harley's shoulder, "No need to be embarrassed by it."

After that, Triston turned to face the rest of us, "Our little Harley here tested at a master's level. He sure is a smart cookie!"

Silence.

"As in . . .a master's degree?" Warren blinked back in shock.

"Yep!" Triston's smile was proud as he ruffled Harley's hair. Harley let out a laugh, but it was a tad bit strained. Harley paused and turned to face us, "Sorry I didn't tell you. It. . . just never came up."

"Harley, that is so-whoa!" Layla exclaimed as she pushed herself up and wrapped her arms around him in a hug. The smile that came onto Harley's lips was small but still very appreciative.

"Yeah, seriously, man, that's amazing!" Jason said as he slung his arm around Harley's shoulders, much like a very, very proud older brother.

"Uh, if you're so smart, then why are you in high school then?" Chase asked, ruining the atmosphere. Both Jake and his clone smacked him.

"Ow!" Chase yelped and rubbed his shoulder, "What? It's a valid question!"

"Could have phrased it a little better, bro." Jake chided as his clone nodded in agreement.

"Oh, no, no! It's okay!" Harley was quick to interject, his hands moving back and forth sharply, "It's fine!"

Harley lowered his hands but didn't fully let them fall to his sides. He seemed to shrink a bit, "I decided to go to high school because I wanted to experience what it would be like to. . .go to a regular school. Triston said it would be okay even though I already had a college degree. . ."

"And as luck would have it, he was pulled from the lottery-like all of you. Though he did hack into our system to put his name in, so the validity of if his name coming up at random is a bit questionable," Triston said with a shrug before adding, "Plus, I did add a twin that wasn't supposed to be here. . .so I would be a hypocrite if I didn't let Harley stay."

Harley scratched his cheek, nervous and bashful, "I never really had an opportunity to go to a normal school and make friends. I was mostly homeschooled, and I skipped so many grades. . . Plus, it was hard to talk to kids my age when they knew how smart I was. Sometimes they just didn't understand what I was saying. I tend to mumble when I get invested in something, so people thought it was weird. . ."

We didn't know what to say to that, so in the end, all we could do was listen to him finish out his thoughts, "But I'm glad I came here, though! I can talk to animals now, and I've made more friends. . . .I have a nice roommate! School has been fun and exciting so far. . .and I feel like I'm going to have a lot of fun going to school with you guys! I hope we have a good four years! Oh, and If you need assistance with homework, I'll help you out!"

"Oh my god, we have to let him have the best childhood ever!" Jake yelled as he raced up to the front to full-on tackle-hug Harley to the ground. Chase wasn't far behind him as he joined in, "We so need to take you on prank runs!"

Will set the hair clip box on the table, got up, and kneeled next to the three of them. His smile was warm, "I. . .also have a good roommate. Though maybe don't bring in any more bats, okay?"

"Those kids don't have good taste," Layla said as she also threw herself into the steadily growing dog pile, "You're a wonderful kid!"

"And it's amazing that you are so smart!" Warren said, clenching his fist in a sort of 'I'm proud of you' pose.

After that, everyone else wanted to get a word in to encourage Harley. Adya threatened to beat up any kid that bothered him. Ethan braved his plant aversion and picked a flower that had appeared next to him to give to Harley. Even Nolan let his lips tilt upward slightly as he said, ". . .have fun."

It was very wholesome and sweet.

God, I love this class.

Harley laid there stunned for a moment, the flower tangled in his coffee-colored hair. His mouth trembled before a smile appeared on his face that could blot out the sun; it was so bright, "I'm so glad I came here!"

Oh, my heart, this kid is gonna kill me one day.

"I know I'm ruining a beautiful moment here," and you actually looked like you regretted speaking up, "But we should finish the lecture. . ."

Triston had tears in his eyes, "Ah, Connor, way to go! It was so nice. . .why'd you have to talk!"

You scowled, "What do you want from me?"

In the end, we did get up to finish the lesson, but if we sat a little closer to Harley after that, it wasn't a bad thing. Once we settled back into learning mode, you started again, "To answer your question, Harley, Semi-voluntary means an aspect of your power is subconscious, and the other is something you have to consciously be doing."

"Ohhhh, that makes sense." Harley said, "But again, it must be rare."

You nodded, "It is. Most powers fall under the 'voluntary category. I only know one person that has a semi-voluntary power. He's our school nurse."

"Oliver?" I choked a little bit in surprise.

"Yes," You said curtly, and I couldn't help but think if Harley had said it instead of me, you would have been so much nicer, "His power 'Healing Touch' stores everything he learned over the years about recovery and cures. So he doesn't have to think about the methods and can just turn on his power to heal people. If his power was involuntary, he would always be glowing."

"So you're saying involuntary powers are always on? You can't turn them off?" Warren asked.

"Yup, if I had to split us up by what we know right now, I would say that Will, Triston, Ethan, Harley, and myself fall under this category. The rest of you have voluntary powers."

Triston was the next one to speak, turning around on his bench to face us, "If you know what your power falls under, it's easier to devise a plan to better control it. Involuntary powers are usually harder to control than voluntary. For example. . ." Triston's eyes roamed the class for a moment before landing on Will, "You can't turn off the mindreading, yeah?"

Will grimaced and touched the cat hair clip in his hair, "No. If it wasn't for this, I would be hearing everyone's thoughts right now."

Triston's face turned a little remorseful, "Sadly, you'll have to learn to not wear them. My daughter said the best way she could figure out to lessen the number of voices is to tune most of them out, kind of like if you were talking to your friends in a crowded cafeteria."

Triston's expression morphed to be more optimistic, "But don't worry, I'm going to help you figure it out! I asked my daughter to give me detailed notes."

Will's face seemed to not know what emotion it wanted to show, but eventually, it became a timid smile, "Thanks."

Triston waved it off, "I would do anything for my students. Do worry too much about it."

"As for the rest of you that have voluntary powers," You crossed your arms, "You merely need to teach your brain when to flip the switch and turn them on and off. Right now, you guys are like a flickering lightbulb because your brain doesn't know what to do, so it just flips the switch at random."

"And once you know how to handle your powers better, you will be able to experiment with them more," Triston added helpfully, "An example of this is, ah, let's say your power might be able to be used on someone else other than yourself. Or maybe you figure out a whole other aspect of the power you didn't know about."

"Like, maybe Warren can also become big?" Harley asked, and Warren froze. The look on his face said that he really shouldn't dare to hope.

"Actually, Harley, that could be something he could do." Triston confirmed, and Warren's mouth formed a little 'o'. I couldn't help but laugh a little at his expression. But, as funny as it was to see him like that, the man had a huge epiphany. I should give him a break.

That doesn't mean I won't tease him later, though.

"Okay, this is getting me excited!" Jake said, "I mean, maybe I can clone myself a hundred times or something, or maybe I could clone other people!"

Chase joined his twin in excitement with a gasp, "I wonder if I could turn anything invisible! Just think of all the things I could sneak into movies!"

Warren couldn't hold it in anymore, his hands flying up to smack both of his cheeks, "I could become big!?"

"Sorry to burst your bubble, but you're going to have to learn how to control it first," You said without sounding sorry at all. The twins deflated at the realization that they will have to do work to get to the fun part. Warren, however, didn't look deterred, a new sort of fire and determination in his eyes.

"But!" Triston was quick to reassure, "Once you get past the basics, it's going to be fun!"

"Let's get started, shall we?" You said, and the smirk on your face was not a good sign.

"Huh?" Triston let out in confusion, "Connor, what are you–"

"You know, Triston, I think I know what will help them along. . ." You tilted your head innocently in a particular direction. . .

"No," Micah said as he sensed the appending doom.

"Wait, wait-" Jason's eyes widened as he too felt the chill in the air.

And their reactions only made the smile on your face grow as you finally said, "I think it's time to turn up the difficulty. Whoever isn't at the obstacle course in three minutes gets detention."

♣ Chapter 10 ♣

"I thought you said we wouldn't be doing this," Warren complained as he looked at the obstacle course with disdain. Everyone was giving Triston the nastiest look we could manage. A group effort that was unplanned but very synchronized.

"Ah. . .well, Connor does make a fair argument. . ." Triston said as he looked on guiltily from where he sat near the edge of the trees, a blanket laid out under him and a drink in his hands. Though I have to say, Triston didn't look as guilty as Will, who awkwardly sat crossed-legged next to him and stared at his offered drink like it was going to come alive and eat his hand. To like, you know, wake up to avenge us, or something.

(We all knew it was better for him to practice his mind-reading away from everyone, but that didn't mean we had to like it, though.)

"Oh, stop complaining," You said, looking unimpressed, "It's not going to be that bad. . .at least not today anyway."

"See, that right there doesn't give us much confidence," Micah pointed out, but you just let out a very Nolan-like sigh. ~~Will you cut it out! God, I hate you.~~

~~You don't.~~

"Okay, fine, I admit I might not be the best human being," Some of us snorted, and you just let it happen. But, to be fair, you must be used to it, "But I do want you to get better. . .Triston and I split the bill every time something gets broken, believe it or not."

Jake and Chase looked at each other, and you must have seen that out of the corner of your eye because you said, "Noted. If you guys break anything on purpose, you'll get points deducted from your next test."

"Aww, lame." Chase sighed.

Jake next to him seemed to have a realization, ". . .so wait, you're saying that Ella was the real trouble maker all along. . ."

Ella blushed to the roots of her hair.

"Hey, don't make fun of her!" Warren came to her defense, but it backfired a bit when he continued with, "She can't help that she always breaks things."

You shook your head as I suddenly got the urge to facepalm, "Today is just a light practice, so don't get too bent out of shape, geez. Jason catch!"

You tossed a quarter from your pocket at Jason, and he fumbled a bit, the coin slipping through his fingers, "You're going to run the course with that stuck to. . . let's go with your forehead. If you let it fall even once, you have to rerun the course. Finish without dropping that, and you're free to go back to the dorm."

Jason stared blankly until you let out a huff, "What are you waiting for? Hurry up and go, or do you want to do this while it's dark?"

Jason shook his head quickly and slapped his palm against his forehead with a loud '*Smack!*' The quarter stuck there for about half a second before it fell to the ground, landing soundlessly in the grass. Chase let out a very satisfying 'pfft,' and Jason made an embarrassed face, bending down and trying again, "Shut up, it's harder than it looks, okay!"

While Jason struggled, you moved on to your next victim, "Kalei, stick out your hand."

Kalei raised an eyebrow but lifted her hand, which you instructed her to make a small fire. The flames faltered a bit in the wind, "Same deal as Jason. Go through the course and don't let the flame go out. Start again if it does. Now go."

Kalei nodded quickly, brought up her other hand to better protect the flame, and started the first obstacle, the balance beam. She paused and turned back around, "Does it have to stay in my hand? Or can I move it to other parts of my body?"

"As long as it doesn't go out, I don't care," You shrugged, and then Kalei was on her way, shifting the flame to the top of her head.

After that, we got similar directions one by one: do something with your power and, if you mess up, go again. The instructions for everyone else were as follows:

> * Jake had to make a clone and drag it along the course with it tied to his ankle or wrist. If it 'poofed,' it was an instant try again.

> * Chase was told to be invisible the whole time, but he had to sing loudly to ensure he wasn't just dipping out and going back to the dorm.

> * Ella was told to just not break anything, making her blush turn at least ten shades

darker. . .but I can't help but think you went easy on her. . .was the door she broke that expensive? Or maybe it was the hole in the wall she caused during the Dodgeball Game from Hell? The world may never know.

* Then you went oddly hard on Micah and told him to shift to a different thing/part/ look whenever he finished an obstacle. So, he couldn't move forward until he changed something about his appearance. But if he changed mid-obstacle, he had to try again. Oof.

* Though Warren wasn't much better, lol. You told him to try to be tiny the whole time and just walk the outside on the course, far enough not to get smooshed, until he reached the end. (Warren: "Dude, do you know how long that's going to take, ugh.") If he became big, he had to stop, become tiny, then continue.

* Adya had to continuously make weapons and toss them aside. When we asked if that was safe, especially with a tiny Warren, Adya had said, 'Eh, I'll try not to cut anyone,' and I swear we all stepped away from her in

perfect unison. Which is pretty funny now that I think about it.

* Ethan had to run the course while trying to keep the nearby plants at bay. Which, to be honest, is not an easy task. . .like at all. Poor Ethan looked like he was going to lose his last ounce of sanity when the first tree branch neared his head.

* Layla had to continuously run laps around the clearing until at least 5 of us finished. . .Which is BIG yikes, honestly.

* Ryuma had to pass through every obstacle, including people, but keep one body part solid. Ryuma chose his right foot. An odd choice because it didn't seem like he could float, and now he was all lopsided. But then again, maybe he had a plan?

* Nolan had to keep a constant glow, it didn't matter what color or how bright. . .

As for what I had to do, it was a three-for-one special. It seemed like you were struggling to come up with an idea for Harley cause the kid was already so good at talking to animals, so you made him assist. And by that, I mean I had to give a surprisingly heavy kid a piggyback ride as I flew a few feet above the course. At the same time, Nolan, the evil and bright monstrosity that he is, was tied to the other end of the rope wrapped around my ankle.

"Nolan, can you go any faster?" I complained as Nolan finally reached the end of the second obstacle. I had to avert my eyes, but it didn't stop me from having to blink away the spots every time I looked his way.

Nolan (I assume) glared at me, "You're the one that chose me! Fuck you."

"No take-backs!" You shouted from where you watched us suffer on Tristion's cozy picnic blanket, sucking down a. . .fruity drink(?), "You had your chance to pick Ella."

"I just didn't want to get super launched or something," I grumbled, and Harley laughed cheekily. I also want to point out that I decided not to choose Ella because she looked like she couldn't handle the pressure after her *cough* incident with a certain dodgeball. I just couldn't do that to the poor girl, so I had to pick Nolan. The lesser of two evils.

At least I got a good view of everyone else struggling, and it wasn't as if Nolan was doing that bad, honestly, compared to some of the others at least. Like, Jason hadn't even started yet, still trying to stick the coin to his forehead, getting more and more frustrated with each press/slap/and plea of 'just please stick c'mon!'. Ryuma kept getting his foot stuck on things, and Micah's face contorted as he tried to get rid of his blue hair.

"I'm not hearing any singing!" You shouted and a smirk formed as you heard Chase curse. Triston chuckled but quickly turned back to Will to continue their session. Will's face took on an uncertain look as he fiddled with his hair clip.

"~We're all in this together.~" Chase bleated out from somewhere in front of me, and I cringed. Why did he have to pick that song out of everything he could have chosen. Maybe it was his way to make the best out of his situation? Either way, I guess we were stuck listening to him sing *High School Musical* songs until the exercise was over.

"Whoa!" Harley whispered in excitement, "You can see so much from up here! Oh, nice to see you again, Henry!"

"Ack!" I let out as Harley waved enthusiastically at a passing bird, jostling me backward. I flew back so hard that Nolan was tugged off the climbing wall and onto his butt.

"Watch it!" Nolan growled as the rope pulled at his arm painfully as he tried to get up.

"Oh, oops, sorry!" Harley yelled. He clung to me harder, and I almost choked from the grip around my neck. Nolan grumbled, and after that, I kinda zoned out a bit. Sure, I was aware when Jason finally yelled out in triumph and all but hopped his way to the balance beam but at the same time, what else was I gonna do but watch everyone? I just had to float there, make sure Harley didn't fall, and wait for Nolan to finish.

My bored brain started doing a play by play like an old-timey announcer:

"Kalei was up first, showing excellent handling of her flames. Oh no! She lost it! What is she going to do now that Chase has seemingly taken the lead! And he has a surprisingly good singing voice, who could have guessed ladies and gentlemen!"

I didn't realize that I was saying that out loud until Harley laughed and continued, "And in a surprising twist, the trio has overtaken Yoshida! He got stuck on the third obstacle! It's anyone's game, folks!"

I looked at him, and he looked at me, and we both simultaneously concluded that this was what we were doing until we went back to the dorm.

Nolan let out a sigh and accepted his fate.

*****

The rest of September and most of October went by, with training and schoolwork blending together. After that first week, we got more used to what our life at Freedom Bay would be like, and slowly but surely, we were getting the hang of our powers. Most of us could at least hold back, like trying not to sneeze, and we were doing a pretty good job, kinda, at keeping our secret from the rest of the students.

There were some close calls, of course. Like the time I was at the beach with Micah and Jason, and the 'wind' picked up our umbrella and sent me flying across the sand like a malfunctioning Mary Poppins. Or the time Jason's hand got stuck to the door of our classroom, and we passed it off as really, really strong glue and teenage stupidity. Or that other time when Ella had ripped off the door to her locker, and we blamed it on a loose screw.

Oh! And the time when Warren suddenly shot up a few inches and whacked his head against the doorway. That day was funny because he yowled like a distressed cat, but then his eyes widened to saucers when he realized what he had just done. Later that day at training, he yowled in despair when he couldn't figure out how he did it.

(Poor Warren.)

All in all, we were getting better. After doing the obstacle course, dodgeball, or any exercise you deemed a 'good teaching method,' we took the rest of the time to test out what we could do and spitball ideas.

Jake had asked if his power was actually semi-voluntary, but we decided it wasn't based on how he wasn't controlling the clone, just making it. We found out he could only make a total of six clones before they started to look janky and that he could only clone himself. He tried with everything he could get his hands on but no dice.

Adya was getting better at the number of weapons she could make but was only able to do basic weaponry, like knives and clubs. But we also saw a determination in her eyes to make something more complex. There was a rumor going around that she was thinking of making a crossbow.

Harley discovered that even though he could talk to animals, not all of them were friendly and wanted to help him. One night, he told me that there was a pet cat from the senior dorms that swore like a sailor and outright refused to talk to 'lowly human scum.' So, Harley's powers could be helpful, but that hinged on if the animal he was talking to wasn't a jerk. Like how can you be mean to Harley of all people? That cat doesn't know what he's missing. . .jerk.

Day by day, Micah got closer to complete transformations. We all theorized that he could probably turn into animals and change what he looked like, but he couldn't become something like a fridge or a car. We passed around the idea that maybe he could harden his body to make it steel, but that idea was quickly tossed out. Also, he couldn't mix animal traits. If he wanted to be a cat, he couldn't grow a dog tail too. By the end of October, he was really good at transforming his body to look like someone else, and it was almost scary how accurate it was when he got around to morphing into me.

Nolan was still functioning primarily as a mood ring, but he figured out how to change the intensity of how bright he glowed and somewhat grasped how to change the color. But if you got him flustered, embarrassed, etc., the color would always depict what he was feeling instead of what he wanted it to be. This only flustered him more, and he was scowling more often than usual after we were done most days.

Ella found a way to sort of hold and release her super-strength until she wanted to break something. That wasn't always a guarantee, though. There was one time she sent Chase flying across the common room and shattered the sliding glass door. It was his fault, really. He shouldn't have embarrassed her so much.

Speaking of Chase, he could make other people invisible with some trial and error, but he had to be touching them to do it. It was also common sense that he could make objects invisible, seeing how we couldn't see his clothes when he disappeared, but they too had to touch him for it to work. It made him a fearsome adversary during the Dodgeball Game from Hell.

Ethan's power was. . .a strange one. You were right in thinking it was an involuntary power, and it was almost like how Harley's worked, but the plants pretty much listened when Ethan told them what to do. Sometimes, they would have a mind of their own and decide to just poke him or mess with his hair. He didn't ask the plants to come alive; they did independently whenever he was around. We thought that maybe Ethan was subconsciously moving the plants and that they weren't, like, actually sentient, but that also begged the question of why he would subconsciously want plants to touch him when he hates them, so we threw that out quickly.

Kalei could control how hot her flames were and how they moved with her mind. She could make multiple fires simultaneously, but the more she lit, the weaker they would become. She had a limited amount of flame she could use. One big inferno or a lot of smaller bursts. We all agreed that she could make her 'storage' larger, and over time it would be like she didn't have a limit at all.

There's not much to say about Jason's, honestly. He's sticky. He can stick to things. But he did figure out how to control it a little better so that he can climb up walls and crawl across ceilings. Also, he could stick to *anything.* That includes liquids. Micah and I almost had a heart attack that one day at the beach when he came out of the ocean looking like a water blob monster. Luckily Micah was quick and pushed him back into the waves before anyone saw him.

Will was getting better at sorting through the noise in his head whenever he took off his hair clip. It still looked like he was physically in pain after about a minute of concentration, but with the help and guidance of Triston and his daughter, he was making real progress.

Speaking of Triston's daughter, we found out that her name was Aspen, and she was in college learning to be a doctor. She had lessons with Oliver on Tuesdays and Thursdays and would swing by to help out when she could. She also told Will to keep the hairclips he borrowed, saying that she was only keeping them for nostalgia and would rather he use them. 'Mind buddies had to stick together, after all,' she had said with a grin.

Will kept the hair clips.

Side note: This was also when I found out that Chase liked girls with dimples.

Ah, who am I forgetting? Oh, Kayla, Warren, and Ryuma.

Kayla was doing WAY better and controlling how long and how fast she could run. Micah had told her his dust devil idea, and later that week, she was making mini tornados for fun. Warren was trying to figure out how he made himself taller, and eventually, he figured it out. He was ecstatic until he realized that there was a sort of time limit to how long he could be small or larger. But Ella had cheered him up, so I guess it wasn't all that bad, haha.

Ryuma found out that he could make other things transparent, living, or otherwise. How he figured that out was a total accident. He was on the balance beam and had tripped, knocking over Adya, and both of them had fallen through the beam and collided with the ground. Ryuma apologized, and Adya was surprisingly chill about the whole thing. Plus, she couldn't wack him anyway, seeing how he was all transparent at the time.

As for me, I figured out that I was controlling the air around me to fly. I also figured out that I could make other things fly if I concentrated hard enough. Back then, I could only lift small objects, like a pen or my notebook. We weren't sure why it was so easy for me to lift myself since I'm way bigger than a pencil, but we figured that I must be subconsciously doing it, while the other stuff I had to think about if I wanted to move.

And while we were figuring out how to handle all the weird changes, we also had to do schoolwork. . .and to say that this was an elite school wasn't a lie. Like, at all. The curriculum was *hard*. Like, REALLY hard. At first, I thought that it was just you making our homework awful on purpose, but after a month here and the whispers of the other grades, I could tell that it wasn't a 'you' thing but a 'Freedom Bay thing. In the end, most of us took up Harley's offer of help at some point.

Except for Nolan.

Because he's stubborn and an idiot.

About a week before Halloween, I couldn't take his frustrated grunts anymore, "Just ask Harley for help, oh my god."

Nolan growled as he aggressively erased what he wrote, the poor eraser almost nonexistent, "No."

"Ah, c'mon man, you know he would be delighted to help you out," I said even though I had already given up on the conversion and was texting Alex on my phone instead.

Nolan angrily threw his pencil down and swung around violently in his desk chair, a neckless coming free from his shirt to land cleanly on his chest, "No!"

I put my phone down and turned to him, mockingly pointing at him, "See, that's why you don't have any friends."

Nolan's hands twitched as if he was debating whether or not to punch me. I waved him off and turned around to lay facing away from him, "Whatever, dude. If you want to have the worst grades in class, be my guest."

I could sense him fuming on the other side of the room and could practically hear him gnashing his teeth. I had gotten used to his brash side, so his anger didn't faze me anymore. I kinda just felt sorry for him, honestly. He couldn't find it in himself to have any other emotion other than anger. It seemed like a terrible way to live.

And a little lonely too.

"Is it a pride thing?" I asked half to be mean, but I must have hit the nail on the head by how Nolan yelled at me to shut up and sent an aurora around the room, mostly an angry red and an embarrassed pink.

I rolled my eyes. I was just about to tell him to stop the light show and that I was going to sleep when his voice floated across the room, almost a whisper, "I can't read."

I spun around so fast I almost hurt my back, "You can't. . .what?"

I must have heard that wrong, right?

Nolan was looking away from me, his fingers digging into his knees, his brown curls glowing a mix of pink and green, embarrassment and jealousy. He spat out his next words quickly, like it physically hurt him to admit weakness, "I can't fucking read normally, okay!? The letters don't cooperate no matter how much I stare at them! How would you feel if you read worse than a fucking ten-year-old!"

Nolan was out of breath, and I stared at him in shock for a moment. The conversation was going so off base that I had a hard time coming up with something to say. This was the first time Nolan had ever really talked about, well, anything. Let alone about himself.

My eyes wandered to his tense muscles, the aggravated twitch of his lips, and I realized he wasn't angry at Harley or the universe for his reading problem. Instead, he was angry with himself for not being able to overcome it. His frustration had boiled to the point that he told *me* of all people. But...what could I say to him? What *should* I say to him?

Finally, I got out, "Dyslexia?"

Nolan's face scrunched up, and he glared at me, his blue eyes blazing, "If you tell anyone, you're dead."

I gave him an unimpressed quirk of my brow, "Okay, Mr. snorts-a-lot."

Nolan gave me a distant look as if he was waiting for me to say more and then let out an annoyed huff when the silence stretched a bit too long. He turned back around to work on his essay, and I stared at his back. His taut and infuriated back. What should I...?

I pursed my lips and knew I would regret ever mentioning what I was going to say next. With a sigh, I sat up, "Since I was sworn into secrecy. . .we could, like, make a deal. You know, to keep your 'oh so precious secret' safe?"

"Huh?" Nolan turned his head to face me, his eyes confused and his mouth in a firm line.

I blew air out harshly, the regret already starting to build but. . . "Ugh. . .I'm pretty good at English, so I could help you. . .when you're having trouble, tutor you, or whatever."

"Why the f- why would you do that?" Nolan asked as he gripped his pencil so hard it looked like he might break it in half. His skin was starting to shine purple, and I faintly wondered what emotion that represented.

I sneered at him, "Because I'm *nice*. You should try it sometime."

Nolan crossed his arms, "And what? How would this deal benefit you exactly?"

Holy shit, he's actually considering it, my brain screamed, but outwardly I shrugged, "I don't know. Maybe you could help me out too. . .I guess. What are you good at?"

Nolan eyed me, gauging whether or not I was insulting him, but eventually relented, "I'm pretty good at math, but I refuse to do word problems."

"Okay," I said as I got up and marched over to him, my hand outstretched for him to shake, "I'll keep your dyslexia a secret and tutor you in English, and in exchange, you'll help me with math or whatever."

The harsh colors lingered on his skin, but he eventually reached out and took my hand, "If you betray me, I'll roast you alive."

"Diddo."

And our unlikely alliance was born.

It wasn't a bad thing.

*****

The rest of October passed, and soon it was Halloween. Freedom bay let us dress up if we wanted to, so the halls were filled with witches, wizards, zombies, the occasional cosplay etc., etc.

I settled into my seat and eyed Micah's cat ears, "Dude, are you sure that's a good idea?"

Micah's whiskers twitched, "I mean, I've been complimented about my 'amazing costume' all day, so I think it will be okay."

I adjusted my pirate's hat, "Uh-huh."

Micah simply shrugged before his eyes lit up slightly, "I like Will's costume. Sherlock Holmes is the bomb."

I tilted my head, "You into mystery novels?"

Micah's cheeks blushed faintly. I was about to say something else, maybe tease him about his nerdy obsession, when Chase accidentally bumped into me, and he let out a quick 'sorry dude!'. I eyed his costume; it was a solid black outfit with a long coat and red gloves. On his face was a white mask covering his eyes, "What's that from?"

Chase smiled and winked, "A video game. The main character is also a Trickster. Haha, get it?"

"Well, you look cool," I said sincerely, making a mental note to check out the game later.

I also seemingly forgot what I would say to Micah because my eyes started to wander to everyone else's costumes. Me the pirate, Micah the cat, Layla the. . .meme?, Nolan the not-celebrater (come on Nolan get in the spirit of things at least once, geez), Jason the spiderman rip off, Will the holmes, I don't know what the hell Adya was wearing (had a lot of belts though), Chase the Trickster, Jake the banana, Ella the witch, Kalei the volleyball Player, Ryuma the zombie (it looked fuckin' cool, he must have spent a lot of time on it), Warren the Captain

America, and finally Ethan wearing a shirt that said 'This is my Halloween shirt.'

And it was at that moment that Harley came sprinting in, just as the bell rang, a huge grin on his face. Once he had his breath back, he stood up straight and then moved his arms in stiff angled movements, "Hello, my fellow humans. Beep, boop."

And. . .Harley, the robot.

It was very adorable, but I couldn't help but let out a loud laugh at what was behind him. Harley tilted his head, a little hurt before he realized our gazes weren't on him, and turned around. Standing in the doorway was our very own teacher. . .in a giant inflatable clown outfit, makeup and all. Through the painted smile on your face, we could see your scowl as the rest of the class lost their shit, laughing.

I took a picture for safekeeping.

"I lost a bet." You said as a way of explanation, almost sounding defensive.

"Who's the clown now, hahaha," Chase belted out, taking off his mask to wipe away the happy tears. And it only got louder when you tried to squeeze through the door but got stuck, your enlarged body not able to pass through.

Harley, who had taken a step back, pursed his lips as you shrugged your way into the classroom.

Finally, he whispered, "Does your nose honk?"

You let out a frustrated huff, reached up, and squeezed your red nose, *'honk!,'* "Yes, now will you sit down? We have a guest speaker today."

It took us a moment to get over the honking sound (because that noise mixed with your expression will *always* be hilarious) before we took in what you said.

"Wait, really?"

You sighed even harder, trying to sit at your desk, but the inflatable suit hindered your progress, "Yes, really. So shut up so she can come in."

"Aww, Connor, I was enjoying the show," said a cheerful voice from the doorway as a middle-aged woman stepped into view. She had her long blonde hair pulled up into a ponytail, and her brown eyes were shining in mirth. Her costume was a weird mix of a ninja and a Viking warrior, and her smile was large and adoringly toothy as she continued, "Oh, well. Guess we can get this started."

Harley scrambled to sit down as she walked into the room, her high heels clicking against the tile floor. Once she got to the front of the class, she spun in a circle, her hair flying. Then, widening her stance and putting her hands on her hips, she proclaimed, "Who's ready to design Vigilante costumes!"

♣ Chapter 11 ♣

The mysterious guest speaker leaned forward, taking in our stunned silence and her smile grew more mischievous, "What am I saying? Of course, you want to! My name's Mrs. McCully, by the way. Nice to finally meet you all!"

You rolled your eyes, which was a thing to see with all the makeup, "Do you have to be so. . .*that?* *Ugh.*"

Mrs. McCully waved you off, not even glancing your way, "Oh, hush, Connor, this is why you don't have a girlfriend."

Oof.

I can feel that punch to your pride from here.

You scowled at her, and I got the strangest urge to pinch your nose to make it honk again. But instead, I asked, "Wait, hold the phone! You're Triston's wife!?"

Mrs. McCully tilted her head, her smile all teeth, "The one and only!"

"Whoa. . ." Jake exhaled as Chase tactfully (Read: not) continued, "But you're so hot!"

Anna's face (I'm tired of writing Mrs. McCully over and over, okay? Leave it alone.) faltered in its brightness before going so bright it was terrifying, "Oh. . .am I Chase?"

"Abort! Abort!" Jake yelled as Chase let out a startled 'Epp!,' and turned invisible, but we could all see his chair fly backward into Kalei's desk (fire erupted on her clenched fingers as she yelled, 'watch it!') and hear the hard thump as he hit the ground.

"You dumbass," Warren huffed angrily as Chase's head (I assume) slammed into Warren's desk, jolting his notebook and pencils to the floor. Chase reappeared, rubbing into his hair with a hissed, "Owwww. . ."

"You deserved that, dude." Jason deadpanned, no sympathy in his voice at all. Nolan pinched the bridge of his nose with so much force I could swear he might have had the intention of breaking his nose to get a one-way trip to the nurse's office and get away from everything. I mean, it worked for me, but I REALLY don't advise doing that because it sucked.

"Pfft," Anna blurted, and all our heads swung back to her as she started laughing full bodily at the front of the classroom, "Triston was right about you guys! Hahaha!"

Anna clutched her stomach, tears forming at the corner of her eyes. The laugh was all wheeze and sounded a bit like a dying cat. The closest thing I can describe it as is a witch's cackle.

"I guess Triston...no both of them, are attracted to crazy?" I whispered mostly to myself, but Jason's hand flew up to his mouth, and he choked on his spit, coughing hard into his hand. If he was drinking water, he might have done a full-on spit take, haha.

"Uuuuuuugggghhh," You groaned loudly, your face making the clown makeup distort as you frowned, "Anna, come on, get your shit together. You're here for a reason, *god*."

Big words coming from you, dude. Just saying.

"Alright, alright, geez." Anna cleared her throat of all her giggles and tried to seem more serious, even with the slight twitch of her lips, "So...who wants to come up here and be the first volunteer?"

Everyone froze. After a few months at Freedom Bay, we had honed our survival instincts, and it was now screaming at us with red flashing lights: 'DANGER! DANGER! DANGER!'. Even Harley was stiff in his seat, and that's saying something.

"Uuuuhhhh. . ." Micah said, the word dragging so long in the silence I couldn't help but cringe a little, biting my thumbnail.

"Oh, don't be like that," Anna said as she leaned against the whiteboard. Again nobody moved, not even Adya (but that probably had more to do with her not caring than being scared of the Viking/ninja warrior threat in front of her. Adya is a different species of girl that I will *never* understand.). After a second, Anna sighed and pointed her finger at us, "K. Gonna just pick then. Eeny, Meeny, Miny, Moe. . .You! Come on down, lucky contestant number one!"

All our heads swiveled to the victim and watched as said victim's blue eyes grew to the size of dinner plates.

Will, the poor soul, pointed at himself, "Me?"

"Yup!" Anna chirped and made the get-over here gesture with her hand, "Hurry on up. We have a lot to cover."

"You got this, Will," Micah said, but his face betrayed him with his wavering smile. I least Micah tried, I guess. Will nodded despite the ever-growing sense of dread that he had to be feeling and got up, pushing his chair back with a squeak. Soon he was at the front of the classroom, and Anna seized his shoulders, holding him firmly in place.

Trapped, with nowhere to run.

I sent him a silent prayer.

"Okay, hun, remind me what your power is?" Anna prodded with a firm squeeze.

"Mind reading." Will blurted out.

"Oh!" Anna exclaimed and spun Will around to face her more fully. Her expression was pure excitement, and her face was a bit too close for comfort, "Just like Aspen!"

"Um, yeah?" Will said awkwardly as he leaned away from her slightly, blinking fast.

Her eyes moved up to his Sherlock Holmes hat, "Hmm, bet you're wearing a clip under the hat, right?"

Will nodded a bit jerkily.

"I see, I see. . .what's your Vigilante name?"

"Um, Deep Dive, ma'am."

"Okay, no, ma'am makes me feel old," Anna said and let his shoulders go. She grabbed a marker and wrote down both his power and his vigilante name on the whiteboard, "Have you thought about your costume at all?"

Will flushed, but he seemed a little more at ease, his body less tense, "A little bit, I guess."

"How about this?" She said as she started to draw on the whiteboard, her movements precise and with intention, "Your power doesn't have much to work with regarding physical strength, which could be a problem in a fight. Sure, you can mind-read their thoughts, but what will you do if you don't have a way to advance? I would recommend a design that takes this into account, being comfortable to move around in but able to hold items . . .Maybe a belt? Pockets? Hmm. Oh, and we don't want to risk a hair clip falling out until you can live without it. . .so I think we need to make a helmet or visor or even a crown that fits snuggly onto your head instead of the hair clip."

As she talked, we watched in awe as she drew her ideas to life. First, a simple human design with a belt around its waist, sketchy additions, and a more complex helmet. Will's mouth was agape before he leaned forward and pointed to the figure's head, "I think a visor or a crown would be better. Not as heavy on my head. Also, I would like the colors to be red and black . . .if that's okay?"

Anna stopped mid-stroke of the marker and said sincerely, "It's your costume, Hun. It can be anything you want. I'm just here to help you bring it to life."

Will paused for a second before he beamed, "Okay."

"I want to go next!" Harley shouted as he practically launched himself out of his seat, waving his arms frantically, "I got so many ideas for my costume! Please?"

"Here," Anna handed Will the marker before turning to the rest of the class, "Alright, pens and paper out everyone. I want you to write down your vigilante name, power, and what ideas you have come up with so far for your costume. Pictures are nice but not required."

There was a scramble as people dug through their belongings to get supplies, and Will looked at the whiteboard makers he had to work with, opting to stay and finish his designs there. I set my notebook on my desk and aligned an array of multiple colored pens. In the background, Anna continued to talk, "Write down anything you want, even if you think it's too outlandish. It might surprise you what we are capable of making here! Considering our engineering and Robotics teacher has plenty of experience and my power can manipulate fabric, we might be able to make almost anything."

"You can manipulate fabric?" Layla perked up, a bright blue marker in her hand, the ink already smudging on her fingers.

"Mmmhmm," Anna hummed proudly before the sleeve of her costume started to flex and change shape. It went from a long sleeve to being scrunched up at her shoulder, as if she had rolled it up herself, "I can move any fabric, no matter how thin or thick it is. I can also compress it down so that nothing can pass through."

"So. . .like your own bulletproof vest?" Adya asked, twirling her pen around in her fingers. She looked highly interested in the conversation now, and I wasn't sure how that would bode well later in the future.

Note to self: stay away from Adya for a little while.

Better not chance death.

"You're the one that can make weapons, right?" Anna asked instead of answering Adya's question right away. Adya grunted in affirmation, and Anna smiled sweetly, "Okay then, come up here and stab me."

Adya blinked in shock, and so did most everyone else in the room. Will had dropped his marker and hastily retrieved it, holding it close to his chest as he took a warry step back from our apparently suicidal guest speaker. Anna just smiled brighter, oblivious of our reactions, "Well, come on!"

You started laughing, slow and maniacally, which is never a good sign, "Yes, yes! Go on, Adya."

Adya's expression shifted from shock to anger real quick, and she scowled. Then, she stood up and marched over to Anna, whose smile was turning quickly into a smirk, and pointed a finger in her face, "Fine. You think you scare me?"

"Hmm, not really," Anna said with a shrug, "Aim at my stomach, okay?"

Eyebrows twitching, and with the whole class simultaneously taking a breath to hold, Adya reached up and pulled a knife from her bicep. Once she had a firm grip, Adya paused, "You really want me to do this?"

"Yep!" Anna tilted her head reassuringly, placing her hand right above her belly button, "Don't worry. Hit me right here."

Adya shrugged, nervousness now gone, "Okay, but you told me to, remember that!"

And without any warning, Adya lunged forward, her deadly weapon aimed perfectly where Mrs. McCully's hand was a second before. My mouth fell open as the blade landed and instantly shattered, the pieces landing on the floor with a sharp cascade of clinking sounds. All that was left in Adya's hand was the hilt, and Adya brought it up to her eye in amazement.

"See, I'm fine! Did that answer your question?" Anna asked as if she didn't just blow everyone's collective minds.

"Holy shit!"

"Whoa!!!!"

"Yoooo!!! That was awesome!!"

As we all shouted and lost our shit Adya looked up, her eyes sparkling, "Teach me your ways."

Anna couldn't hold it in anymore, and the wheezing, dying cat laugh was back in full force. "Sure thing! Best class ever! Hahaha-wheeze-hahaha!"

You leaned back in your chair and crossed your arms as best you could in the clown suit. Your expression was almost, dare I say, fond, "Brings back old times."

"Okay, okay, enough fun and games. We really got to focus now. Will, be careful of the shards until I come back with a broom. Everyone else, start brainstorming. I will be right back!" Anna shouted as she hustled out the door, pointing at everyone before disappearing altogether.

It took us a few minutes to get a hold of ourselves and settle back at our desks but eventually, it became quiet again. . .

"So, she's crazy, right?"

"Oh, yeah, definitely."

Jason choked on his spit.

*****

The rest of the week, we were all pulled from class, one at a time, to talk to Mrs. McCully about our costumes. Anna made us draw lots for our order, and I was the fifth from the last to meet up with her. So on a Thursday morning in November, Anna popped her head in after her session with Ella and asked, "Okay, Skylar, you ready?"

Nolan's hand froze above the group assignment we were doing for the book *Lord of the flies*. (By the way, why the heck did you make us read that? It was total nightmare fuel. Like they were gonna put a kid's head on a stick! Oh. My. God. I just realized you made *Harley* read that! You're a monster! I literally can't get over this realization wtf.) I nudged Nolan's foot and quickly wrote, 'I'll help you later!' as I said, "Yep! Let me just. . .okay done!"

Nolan's expression was neutral as I gathered my backpack and threw it over my shoulder, but I knew he was panicking inside. As Anna closed the door behind me, I thought that I'll have to be extra nice to him today. Especially if he gets called on by you, the demon teacher because I knew that would instantly ruin his day.

I was a few steps behind Anna as she strolled the halls wearing a pair of mom jeans and a blue long sleeve shirt. It kind of felt weird seeing her in regular clothes. Not that I expected her to wear a ninja/Viking outfit all the time, but first impressions are hard to override, you know?

I watched her long hair sway across her back as I followed her to the second floor to the Home Ec. classroom. Anna pulled open the door, and I was greeted by two other teachers. I knew one from my cooking class, Mrs. Briar, a bustier woman with her brown hair styled in a bob. The other one was a man wearing wrangler work pants and a maroon shirt. He also had a smudge of grease on his cheek, and I wondered if it was recent or if everyone decided not to tell him.

"You have grease on your cheek," I said because I figured at least someone had to tell the poor man if it wasn't intentional. His thick eyebrows scrunched up, and he scrubbed hard with his fingers under his eye. They came away black.

"Were you guys ever going to tell me?" He asked, exasperated as Anna gently pushed me into the room and gestured to the only empty seat at the table.

Mrs. Briar, Emily, smiled, "Ah, well. . ."

Anna shrugged as she sat on the edge of the table, "We figured you knew about it."

"How would I know about it! And why would I leave there deliberately!?" Mr. Wilson, Brad, shouted before he pinched his nose hard, "Oh, whatever! I don't care."

Brad let out a long breath to calm himself before he shifted in his seat to face me, "So, Skylar, how are you?"

"Uh, good. I think?" I said awkwardly when everyone stared at me, all at once.

"Your power is flight if I remember, right?" Emily asked as she shuffled a few papers around, "How does it work?"

I felt a bit like I was being interviewed for a job. Kind of weird because I'd never had a job before, but I answered her question anyway, "I move the air around me to fly, and, uh, I can move small objects around too."

"Okay," Brad said as he leaned forward, his face rigid but not unwelcoming, "Want to show us what ideas you've got so far?"

"Sure," I said as I dug through my bag for my notes. They were a bit crumpled when I shoved them quickly in my bag this morning, so I had to straighten them out on the table. I had almost forgotten them altogether because I had been adding ideas down late into the night and left them on my desk in the dorm. I had to run back in a rush and almost didn't make it to class on time—story of my life right there. (I know. The irony is funny. Ha. Ha. Ha.)

There were three pages in total. One was my best attempt at drawing what I wanted my costume to look like, the second was gadgets I wanted to include, and the final was a list of ideas.

Bradley whistles, "Way to come prepared, kid."

I blushed, rubbing my neck, "I was excited."

"It's not a bad thing," Anna said with a giggle. She hopped off the table and leaned over my shoulder to see what I wrote, "Hmm. . ."

She reached over to grab a blank piece of paper and started to sketch a better version of my crude design, "I like the thought of making your costume able to reflect where you are. It's stealthy. Brad, do you think you could make a helmet that retracts, so it's not always in the way?"

"Oh, definitely," Brad replied as he grabbed his own paper, "Or do you think it would be better to have a visor? It would be more compact."

"We also have to take into account that we

don't want his vision to be too blocked, or he might run into things." Mrs. Briar put in helpfully.

"I think I like goggles the best," I spoke up, "It's simple but effective."

"Okay, goggles it is. For the boots, do you want to give yourself a speed boost or help you stabilize yourself?" Anna asked as she drew a pair of goggles next to her sketch and pointed the pencil's eraser at my drawing's large blocky shoes.

"I was thinking. . .both? Is that possible?" I asked, a little taken aback by how fast this conversion was going. I guess they did have plenty of practice from my other classmates before me. Still a little jarring, though.

"I'll see what I can come up with," Brad said as Mrs. Briar tilted her head, "How do you feel about a color scheme of blue and white?"

"That's okay."

"A cape?"

I grimaced as I thought about that one movie where too many people died because they wore a cape, "No capes, please."

"Noted. No capes."

The meeting went like that for about thirty minutes as we bounced around ideas and erased and redrawn sketches until everyone at the table was satisfied. I stared at the final design. Blue and white, boots that will help me stabilize in the air and work like a jet booster, goggles that match the color of my hair, a detachable sling on the back that could hold whatever weapons I chose, and hidden pockets and belts for anything else I wanted to add on.

It was so cool I could have cried on the spot. And I think the adults around me could see that as they all gave me fond looks, Brad going as far as to pat me on the head. Now all I had to do was wait until Anna, and the rest made the costume, promising that I would have it before winter break.

I was vibrating in excitement all the way back to class and the rest of the day after that.

December couldn't come soon enough.

*****

That night Nolan and I sat on our dorm floor, papers spread out around chaotically, but not enough for us to not know where everything was. Since I was gone for pretty much the whole period, we were trying to catch up. It was going fine until my dumb mouth decided to say, "Man, why is this so hard? It would be so much easier if we'd just asked Harley."

I winced in instant regret.

Nolan let out a shout of frustration and threw his pencil across the room. He flung up his arms with a groan and fell backward hard on the floor before turning away from me.

Um. . .oops?

Gah, I'm an idiot.

"Maybe we should take a break," I said with a cringe, unsure how to dodge the minefield I created. I got up from the floor, backing away slightly, "I'm going to get a soda. Do you want anything?"

Nolan flopped on his back and turned his head to give me an irritated look as he spat out, "Why does life suck!"

I froze because:

What the hell do I say to that!?

"Um, buddy, you. . .okay?" I asked gently, trying not to poke the bear and get mauled for my efforts. As much as our relationship (partnership?) had deepened over the mouths, I still felt like I had to walk on eggshells around him. Not because I was scared or angry or pitied him or anything like that, but because I just didn't want to ruin what we had. It took a lot of work to get here, and I didn't want it to disappear because I'm an idiot that doesn't have a filter.

And because. . .Nolan was my friend.

A very bitchy friend but a friend all the same.

And I always take care of my friends.

Nolan looked back at the ceiling, his skin flashing through so many colors it was hard to keep track. His mouth scrunched angrily before he just. . .deflated, going slack. He unclenched his fists and placed them flat on the ground, fingers flexing across the hardwood. I waited patiently, deciding it was too dangerous to move yet.

Finally, after a small defeated sigh, he said, "It's the anniversary."

Okay. I can work with this. Slow and steady now, don't speak too fast, "Anniversary?"

Nolan shifted away from me, his next sentence muffled as if he was pressing his lips to the floor, "The anniversary of. . .my mom died last year. Car crash."

"Oh," I said, taken aback. I prepared for anger. I prepared for him being a little snippy. But this? I didn't know what to do. My brain failed to come up with something to say, but I managed to sincerely get out, "I'm sorry."

The silence stretched out for a long time. Nolan didn't move, and I stood there awkwardly by the door, not sure if I should leave him alone or comfort him. I suspected so many things for him to say, all of them over-dramatic and mean, but now the air was just sad and depressing.

I had to say *something*, or I was going to go crazy, "Do you. . .do you want me to leave you alone?"

"Not really," The words came out choked, and I panicked.

"Oh my god, don't cry, please!" I all but yelled, gesturing wildly and looking around the room as if the answer to my problem would be written on the walls, "Um, UM! I don't know what to do! AH, Do you want a hug? No, that's weird, isn't it! Sorry, I said anything! Oh, I'm making it worse, aren't I!"

I didn't notice Nolan turning to face me as I stumbled over my words, but I did hear him say, "You're terrible at this."

I paused mid gesture to look down at him. His face wasn't sad or angry or frustrated. It looked more tired than anything, his eyes slightly red. He pursed his lips in thought before he pushed himself up with effort and reached into his shirt, pulling out a locket, "Come here, you idiot."

Given the situation, I decided to let the idiot comment slide and promptly sat down next to him. He gave me a sideways look before prying the locket open. Inside was an old picture that looked well-loved, of a woman with long curly brown hair. The photo was taken mid-laugh, her face bright and happy, her hazel eyes crinkling in joy. Nolan pressed a finger against the protective glass, gently gliding around her face before he clutched the locket close, "I miss her."

"She was pretty," I said, and Nolan let out a huff of air beside me. Worried that I had accidentally offended him, I turned to apologize, but Nolan waved me off, closing the locket with a click and tucking it back under his shirt.

We sat in silence for a while, and I wasn't sure how to break it. This is the most Nolan has ever told me about himself, at least in a personal way. I didn't want to upset him, but at the same time, this was a sort of progress that I never would have foreseen. So, biting my lip and hoping that I wouldn't screw this up, I said, "Thank you for telling me. . ."

Nolan hummed and got stiffly to his feet, shoved his hands into the pockets of his sweats. He started walking to the door and paused to look back when I didn't move, sure that I said the wrong thing, "Weren't you going to get a soda?"

I blinked at him, and Nolan scrunched up his nose in irritation, "If you want to sit there, be my guess, but I'm leaving."

And without saying another word, he pushed open the door and disappeared; our bonding moment over.

I did the only thing I could do:

I went downstairs and grabbed a soda.

And if I didn't see Nolan until the next day, I didn't mention it.

*****

The end-of-semester exams were hell on earth.

The final week before winter break was spent doing exam after exam after exam until my eyes hurt, and my fingers were cramping from writing so much. And it wasn't as if anyone could relax after school was over because you were going extra hard on training, and we all would end up coming back to the dorms well after dark, tired and covered in bruises. I was almost grateful when we finally, *finally,* got to our very last exam:

Vigilante studies.

Just one more, and we would be free. Winter break was so close, but oh so far.

We had gotten our costumes the week before, and now we're ready for anything you had to throw at us.

"Okay," You said with a sugary sweet smile, "Who's ready for this?"

Everyone looked at each other and remained silent.

"Ugh, fine, way to take the fun out of it," You groaned, "The exam is going to be split into three sections. One: fighting. Two: overall growth of your powers. And three, my favorite, a written portion."

I let out a groan of despair, and it was contagious because soon, everyone followed my lead. The smirk you gave us was a new kind of evil, "Don't worry! I'm gonna let you pick what you want to do first-"

"WEEE WOOOO! WEEEE WOOOO!"

We were all thrown off when the siren sounded so loud that my ears rang. The smirk fell off your face, your shoulders tensing, "Shit!"

I brought my hands up to my ears and could barely hear Warren over the blare of the alarm, "What the hell is that!?"

"Shut up!" You snarled as you pulled out your phone, "Nobody move! Got it!"

Everyone was taken aback by how forceful you were. Sure, you are mean-spirited, but you never actually yelled at us like that before. Harley scooched closer to me, his eyes wide.

After looking through your phone, you slammed it into the ground with a loud shout of, "Fuck!"

You took a deep breath to steady yourself before turning to us and saying, so seriously, it was terrifying, "We have to go."

"What's going on?" Kalei asked as you started to push us toward the edge of the forest, towards the dock at the back of the island.

You steered us harder, "We don't have time for this! A Superhero is attacking the school! We have to *go!*

☁ Chapter 12 ☁

The sirens cut off abruptly, mid-blare, about two minutes into our rushed scramble to the back of the island. But, honestly, even though the sound assaulted my head as I ran, I barely took notice when it stopped. My thoughts were a jumbled mess, a neverending echo of:

A Superhero is attacking the school.

A Superhero. . .is attacking the school.

A Superhero is attacking the school!!

And my teenage brain didn't fully know how to process that, you know? Like, I've seen fights on TV, and there have been attacks near me. . .but it's never been that close to home. And yes, I know I was training for this but at the same time. . .

It's a bit scary, right?

My thoughts were still swirling around in my head as we scrambled out of the treeline. I bent over to catch my breath, breathing hard and staring at my boots as they sunk into the sand of the beach.

In and out.

In and out.

Then:

"Oh, thank god, at least you guys got away!"

And there was Oliver, his eyes wide, dried blood coating his hair and trailing down his right cheek. His fingers loosened around the baseball bat he was clutching in a death grip, and it slipped from his hand and hit the dock with a *'thunk.'* With a bit of a wobbly smile, Oliver left the bat behind and stumbled over to us, his legs weak in relief. The red in his hair matched the slowly darkening sky behind him, and I couldn't stop staring at how it matted his curls...

...Oh god, there was so much blood...

"Jesus," You cursed as Oliver bent in front of you, out of breath, "Are you the only one that got out?"

Still shaky on his feet, Oliver grabbed your shoulders and squeezed, "They incapacitated...all of the teachers. I barely got out of there...and turned on the alarms. It's bad, Connor."

You took a shaky breath, "And the other kids?"

We all waited with bated breath for his answer, our shoulders tense. I was still staring at the dried blood coating half of Oliver's face and the roots of his hair. Oliver's expression was worried, but the sharp edges of fear softened slightly, "They're okay, for now. The superheroes are keeping everyone in the main courtyard. . .but Connor. . .you should know that. . ."

Oliver grimaced before he let out a long trembling breath of air:

"Connor, it's Anna."

Your hands dropped from Oliver's shoulders in shock, "What?"

My mouth fell open when I realized what Oliver just said, but I wasn't the one who spoke up. I was too shocked.

"The principal's wife?" Layla squeaked, and everyone who hadn't made the connection yet gasped, "Is she okay!?"

Oliver's eyes scrunched up in bitter regret, "No, you don't *understand. It's Anna.* She's the one attacking the school. She took out Triston first. . ."

The silence that followed that statement was deafening. The only sounds were the water lapping at the shore and the wind blowing your hair out of your face, revealing your total and utter shock. Then, your expression slowly moved to anger, and you clenched your fists, "*What?* You can't be serious.

There's just no way she would do that! I've known her since we were kids!"

Nobody knew what to do. It was maybe thirty minutes ago that our only worry was the written portion of an exam. Everything was escalating so quickly that it made my head spin, and I could barely register that Oliver just looked sad, "I *am* serious, Connor. I'm sorry."

You and Oliver shared a long look until you pursed your lips, angry but resigned, "Okay. . .okay. One thing at a time. Did you call anyone? José? Angela?"

Oliver shook his head, "No. Emily and Anna are working together. She blocked transmissions with her technopathy. I tried to start one of the boats, but they've all been siphoned beforehand. The helicopter is a no-go too. They must have been planning this for a long time, Connor. We have to-!"

"Ohhhhhhhh, we have to fight, don't we?" Harley said matter of factly, and everyone swung their head in his direction, shocked.

Your furrowed your eyebrows as Oliver stared owlishly in surprise behind you, "No, absolutely not. I can't believe-!"

Harley blinked rapidly in response, "Did I say something weird?"

And at that moment, everything came rushing up, emotions swirled around in my head, and my heart and I blurted, "Why not?"

Now it was my turn to get the full brunt of everyone's stares, but I didn't regret saying what I did. I knew what I needed to do. Your stare was the hardest of all, and sure I might have been irrationally scared that you were gonna wack some sense into me, but I went on anyway, "Why not fight back?"

Your jaw dropped.

Everyone looked at each other, shifting in place. Adya interrupted the silence by tilting her head slightly, her smile growing a little bit deranged, "Haha, Dork's got a point! Why not? Let's kick some superhero ass!"

Ryuma was the next to speak, his voice firm and his posture straight in his all-black costume, stepping past a still spooked Jason, "And no one's coming to help, yes? Let's fight."

Ella bit her lip and timidly pulled at the tip of her braid as she added, "This is what we were training for, right? We are trying to be vigilantes. . ."

"No!" You spat out, throwing your arms in the air in exasperation, "No! We have a plan for this-"

Warren stood up straighter and slammed his fist against his chest, the steel studs embedded in the knuckles of his gloves reflecting the light of the sun, "Yeah! Why are we acting like cowards right now? We have to save our school!"

"Oh, I'm not a coward, right bro?" Chase smirked as he threw his arm over his brother's shoulder, his eyes gleaming from behind his white mask.

Jake was quick to reply, crossing his arms over the large 'BD' embroidered on his chest, "Quite, dear brother of mine. Our time has come."

"We did just get our costumes, so we are dressed for the occasion," Micah shrugged as he also stepped forward into the growing mass of teenage rebellion, fiddling with the green cuffs on his sleeves.

You let out a groan that mainly turned into a growl as you pulled aggressively at your eyelids in frustration as more and more of us yelled our cooperation for this new turn of events. When Kalei dramatically raised a fist of fire to the darkening sky and Nolan begrudgingly agreed with a roll of his eyes, Oliver laughed, placing a hand on your shoulder, "You taught them well."

"Oh, shut up. . .fine! Fine!" You said as you too joined the circle, Oliver happily trailing behind to join as well, "But if we are doing this, we need a plan. Don't fucking go in and get yourselves killed. God."

"Alright, Teach has joined the party!" Jake smirked, "Aww, I didn't know you were capable of caring! I'm touched."

Ouch. . .hahaha.

You pinched the bridge of your nose, "If this wasn't a life or death situation, I would be giving you so many detentions right now, you brat."

"Fair enough."

"Okay, guys, let's totally focus right now," Layla said as she flung out her gloves, the pink matching her boots and meshing nicely with her light blue pants and crop top, "Even though this is kinda cool, we have to be mature about this!"

"Let's go over what we know so far," Kalei started calmly, raising her hand and putting down a finger with each point, "Mrs. Briar and Mrs. McCully attacked the school. Help's not coming, and we can't escape. . Anna can control fabric, and Emily can control electronics. The other teachers aren't going to be able to help. . ."

"They have the other students tied up in the courtyard, in one big group," Oliver was quick to add, "All the other teachers are there too."

"So we need to figure out a way to sneak back, fight Tristion's crazy wife, and rescue everyone. Shouldn't it be easy because of our numbers?" Warren said, his hand on his chin in thought.

You shook your head, "Don't underestimate Anna. She may look all nice and bubbly, but I've seen a vicious side of her. . .which, I guess, makes sense now."

You cringed, and I honestly felt bad for you. The thought of someone close to me, like Jamie or Alex, becoming evil and hurting my friends turned my stomach. That would suck no matter who you were.

"Plus, we can't just go in guns blazing," Will pointed out, his blue-tinted visor glinting in the dying light of the sunset, "We have to make sure nobody gets hurt."

"Hmm, we just have to take into account everyone's strong suits, make sure the configuration works with everyone..." Harley mumbled, lost in thought.

"I could go underground?" Ryuma suggested, "Grab her before she acts?"

"Maybe, but that's too dangerous. What would we do after that?"

"Maybe a distraction to lead them away?" Harley was drowned out a bit because of how quiet he was.

"If anyone is injured, you have to bring them to me," Oliver said, determination shining in his eyes, "We could set up an evacuation location. Maybe the beach?"

"The fountain. . ." Harley whispered.

"I could stab her?" Adya said, and we turned to her, our faces all showing our collective thought of *really, Adya?*.

"What? It would stop her, wouldn't it?" Adya said defensively.

"Vigilantes don't kill people!" Micah shouted, "That's, like, rule number one!"

"Okay, I'll only stab her a little, geez." Adya shrugged her shoulders and crossed her arms over her bandaged chest. It was at that moment that I finally noticed she had a belly button piercing. When the hell did she get that!? At least it matched her outfit, though.

"No! No stabbing!"

"Eureka!" Harley shouted in happiness, so loud it drowned out everyone else, slamming his fist into his palm, "It's perfect!"

"What's perfect?" Jason asked, his face scrunching curiously behind the black mask around his eyes and his hair sticking up in every direction. Huh, now that I'm thinking about it, he styled it himself, which was *a choice.* Maybe he wanted that bad boy look with a dash of gentlemanly charm for his outfit? You know, given that he looks a bit like a phantom thief, that would totally steal your car and also your girl too.

I went on a weird tangent there, didn't I? Anyway, back to Harley:

"The perfect plan!" Harley gushed excitedly, "Everyone is involved, we save the day, and everything works out in the end. Perfect!"

Your eyes narrowed in irritation, "You really thought this through. . ."

Harley nodded furiously, "Yep!"

"Well, lay it on us, little man, don't leave us hanging," Jake said, putting a hand on Harley's shoulder in a brotherly way. Hmm, I wonder if Chase ever gets jealous. But that's a line of thought for another day.

"Okay!" Harley said with so much determination it was adorable, "So this is what I came up with. . ."

*****

Hands gripped my shoulders harshly as I flew slowly through the forest, high in the treetops. My outfit was as dark as the sky around me, reflecting the cluster of stars in the Milky Way. I groaned when the fingers dug deeper because I had to swiftly dodge a tree. . .that I almost ran into because SOMEONE distracted me by trying to mutilate my delicate collarbones, "God if I knew you would have freaked out this much, I would have asked Harley to choose someone else. Ow!"

Nolan growled and only clung to me harder, "You think I like this, depending on a total idiot to not drop me from three stories in the air and to my death?"

I scoffed, "You wouldn't die. . .probably."

"Probably! Why is it always *you*," Nolan grumbled, and I wasn't sure what to say as a snappy comeback, so I settled with, "Oh, I'm so not helping you with our next book report, mark my words."

"You wouldn't dare!"

"Shh!" I interrupted his highly predictable rant, "We're almost there. You're gonna give us away!"

I got so used to Nolan's mannerisms at that point that I knew he was clenching his teeth to hold back a retort. I mentally put another point on our imaginary scoreboard: Skylar 28 - Nolan 32. Don't ask me why Nolan was winning, I would rather not talk about it, thanks.

I slowly adjusted one of the higher branches to get a better look at the courtyard. Oliver had told us as much as he could, and it looked like he was accurate in his descriptions. Surrounding the tiny fountain was a mass of students, arms tied behind their backs by fabric. The area was illuminated by the fancy lamp posts that Triston liked to brag that his daughter picked out in the recent renovations. I could see that the teachers were also there, tied up more harshly than the students were.

And in the middle of it all were Anna, Emily, and Triston. The man looked like he was still unconscious, lying on his side with his arms and legs tied that harshest of all, a cloth sealing his mouth shut. The superheroes were dressed for the role, but I definitely could tell it was them under the masks and body armor, Anna's long blonde hair a dead giveaway.

"Fuck," Nolan whispered, and I couldn't help but agree. I took a steadying breath, trying to calm the nerves welling up, and whispered back, "I'm going higher."

Nolan's arms wrapped around me in answer, and I slowly ascended. Out of the corner of my eye, I saw Jason and Ella creeping up to the back of the main building to get in position, large duffle bags on their shoulders. Ella grabbed all the bags to carry herself and clung to Jason's back as he crawled up the wall and to the roof. Then they started to get to work on setting up their end of the plan.

"Are you ready for this?" Nolan suddenly asked. He cursed as I lost control for a second and tilted to the side. Luckily I was able to suppress my yelp in time, no thanks to Nolan. I righted myself as I eyed Jason crawling back down the wall to get his second passenger. I let out a breath as Will joined, making the group of two into three, "What about you. Think you got all the colors sorted out?"

"Of course I do!" Nolan snarled, and for a long second, I could feel the muscles of his arms tense, "I have to, don't I?"

"You got this," I said sincerely.

"I don't need your encouragement, gross." Nolan barked back in utter disgust.

"Shh!" I said more to be mean than the worry of getting caught. Nolan huffed, and I knew he just had to be rolling his eyes. I swear one day they'll roll right out of his head. I looked at the large clock embedded above the entryway to the main building: 9:58 pm.

Two more minutes. Deep breaths, Sky, you got this. And just in time, I saw the side door closest to me mysteriously open and close. On the rooftop, Will's head turned until he was looking right at me. He seemed to be readying himself before he reached up to the visor snuggled around his head, and at the moment, I knew it was time.

I gripped Nolan's arm, "Ready?"

". . .yes."

And at ten o'clock on the dot, I flew out of our hiding, Nolan hanging off my back like a koala, and yelled, "Evildoer, I have come to stop you!"

Nolan's groan was drowned out by the sound of epic battle music suddenly coming out of every speaker of the school's sound system. If I wasn't on a critical mission, that would have made me pause because Chase was just supposed to turn the alarms back on, not blast hardcore beats.

But you know what?

Chase, you madman, you're perfect the way you are, never change.

Either way, the music, and my dramatic reveal had their desired effect. Students, teachers, and superheroes alike were startled and looked around in shock. Taking advantage of the disarray, I launched myself into the next part of the plan, literally. Flying straight toward the enemy, as fast as I could manage without messing it up and accidentally going off course, I spun around at the last second so that Nolan was facing Emily and Anna directly. I clenched my eyes shut, but even with my eyes protected by my tinted goggles, the light that Nolan emitted from his body was so bright it stung.

I heard Anna yell out in shock, and I blinked open my eyes to see Warren landing a punch and Emily suddenly getting attacked by a large bird, screeching.

Nolan gripped my shoulders, "Fly, you dolt!"

"Right!" I said as I flew up to the roof where Jason was shooting small objects out of a t-shirt gun to distract or directly hit the enemy (primarily balls, packets of paint, and occasionally confetti). Ella was grabbing her own ammo from one of the duffle bags for her to throw with her super-strength. Will's arms were shaking slightly, his knuckles white from gripping the lip of the roof. He was taking quick breaths, his face scrunched up. I landed next to him, and Nolan jumped off my back, "Are you doing okay?"

Will's voice was a little strained, but it did have an air of confidence to it, "Yes. Go. Nolan, green."

The top of the roof lit up a bright green, shining like a giant neon sign. We all settled on the color meanings beforehand. Harley said that since Mrs. Briar could control electronics, we needed a way to communicate between the groups that didn't rely on technology. Will would tell Nolan what color to glow, and we would consider that as we fought. It was a big thing to ask of Will, we knew, but he was the only one that could listen to all of us, even if it's distorted by all the other thoughts that had to be slamming into his brain from all the frightened students.

The color green means to start the rescue part of the plan. I jumped off the roof and watched as Ryu, Layla, and five clones (plus the original Jake) ran out of their hiding place and towards the captured students. Layla used her super-speed to grab the closest student in a bridal carry and haul them off to the safe zone we set up on the football field (Oliver was stationed there to heal any injury). Ryu sunk into the ground only to reappear next to a startled student or teacher and grab their wrist to bring them down with him. Jake was using his clones in a sort of bodyguard formation, pulling student after student to their feet and leading them out of the courtyard.

But my focus was on the intense battle that was taking place next to the tiny fountain. Layla had rushed forward and grabbed Triston at the start of the rescue, so the fighting team was going all out. But even though Kalei, Adya, Warren, Harley, Ethan, Micah, and eventually me were fighting Anna, she was powerful. She batted away the projectiles that Jason and Ella were sending with ease as if it was an annoying fly rather than a precision attack. So you were right to say not to underestimate her.

Damn, she was *vicious.*

Even though there were no electronics around her, Mrs. Briar was holding her own too. I remembered hearing from Brad that she grew up taking multiple self-defense and martial arts classes, and her skills were showing. She flung Adya back and blocked an attack from Warren, who suddenly popped up big beside her. She only lost focus when a bright blue cat jumped from the top of the fountain and clung to her head. She growled, grabbing the creature and chucking it away from her. Micah shifted back midair and landed on his feet as if he was still a cat.

Kalei went for a punch, her fist covered in blue flames, and Anna dodged easily. Unconcerned, Anna let out a bright laugh when Ethan launched a large root out of the ground at her, dirt landing in his hair as he scowled, "Haha, you *do* hate dirt!"

And it came to me then, the realization that she knew *everything* about us. We told her about the powers during the design sessions and how our costumes worked; where all of our built-in trump cards were. Nevermind that Triston probably told her so much about his passion project, about his little ragtag class of vigilantes that he stitched together by pulling names out of a hat.

Would it always be like that once we, if we, turned into actual vigilantes? Fame was a double-edged sword, and that fact hit me like a truck.

I landed with a bit of a stumble and cursed. Just a little longer, I thought as I flew to the side to avoid Anna sending a part of her sleeve at me like a whip. Just a little longer until Nolan shined a bright white.

Come on, you can do this.

You're going to be a vigilante.

You're going to *save people.*

I barely registered Ella jumping off the roof, cracking the cement when she landed and joined the fight. Jason was quick to follow after her, climbing down the wall as fast as he could.

Their ammo was now gone; no more distractions were left.

I looked up, taking in the chaos around us. . . taking in the fact that we were *losing.*

But then it finally happened:

Nolan glowed white, and the earth shook.

The ground started to move, and Chase popped into existence in the fountain, his body soaked with water and a smirk on his face. Everyone jumped back, and I grabbed Kalei and Ethan on the way, snagging the back of their outfits and dragging them away. For a moment, Mrs. Briar and Anna were there, then they let out a yell as the footing literally disappeared under them and then fell, sliding at an almost 70-degree angle and into a slide. . .

Gone.

There was a breath of silence through the blaring of the epic music playlist that Mrs. Briar was too occupied to turn off, and then the remaining students in the courtyard cheered. The sound echoed off the buildings, but I knew it was too soon to celebrate, the battle not yet over.

Adya quickly followed the enemy, jumping heroically into the slide as if she was doing a cannonball into a pool. Warren was next, skidding to a stop with the skates in his shoes retracting before he jumped. Then it was Harley with an adorable laugh of joy, Micah with determination, Kalei with her badass energy, Ethan with no emotions on his features, Ella and Jason at the same time because she stumbled and barreled into him. . .

I hesitated for just a second to say to the crowd of happy students, "Evacuate to the football field. Shooting Star, Yuurei, and Body Double are here to help you."

"Got that right!" Layla smiled, and she hefted up a brightly blushing boy, his eyes wide in awe.

Jake patted himself on his multiple backs and loudly proclaimed that Body double is indeed there to help.

Ryuma appeared with Nolan and Will, their transparent bodies becoming whole and lightly landing on the concrete. Will clumsily reached up the button on his visor, sighed in relief, and then subsequently collapsed.

I shot forward to help, but Nolan just gave me a look as he held onto Will's limp arms, "What are you doing? I got him; go fight, you idiot."

I nodded, and then I, too, jumped into the slide. I came out faster this time around, shooting out like a ball in a pitching machine. I yelped as I barely stopped myself from splattering against the far wall. I spun around to see the damage of the battle, and my jaw dropped.

My mind ground to a halt as I took what exactly I was seeing, slowly descending, so I was next to an equally gobsmacked Warren. I just couldn't believe what I was seeing, the adrenaline in my body making me twitchy, and I stared for a long time without really seeing.

Sitting on a makeshift stage with a table covered in party food and a large banner with red font saying 'CONGRATULATIONS!' was none other than Tristion McCully.

Triston clapped his hands with a smile, "I'm so proud of you!"

Beside him, you pulled at the party popper in your hand, and a small handful of confetti fell to your feet when it popped. You let out a very unenthusiastic, "Yay."

Then (Then!) Anna McCully stepped up next to her husband and kissed his cheek, "That was fun. We should do this next year."

I couldn't hold it in anymore, "What!?"

"Sorry, hun, for trickin' ya," Mrs. Briar said as she put what I think is a Japanese Dango in her mouth, "You did really well!"

I was speechless, utterly speechless. Nolan would have died of shock if he saw how speechless I was.

"Can someone explain what the hell is going on?" Warren broke his spell before me, stepping forward.

Harley tilted his head in confusion, "Wait, you guys didn't know it was the exam?"

And that's when my soul left my body.

*****

Only when everyone else, including Oliver with a way too innocent smile, was gathered together did you decide to explain, "Yep, Harley put the pieces together: that was your final exam. I'm so annoyed that he figured it out early. . ."

"Ah," Harley said bashfully, "I'm sorry."

"Don't you apologize to the lunatic," Jason harshly scolded, protectively yanking Harley away, much to the poor kid's confusion. Other than that, though, none of us moved from our irritated/still slightly shocked posture, our arms crossed and scowls a plenty.

Triston let out a laugh despite our disapproving looks and grabbed Anna's hand, "You didn't think my sweet and beautiful Anna could be a villain, did you?"

"Well, obviously we did!" Nolan ranted, his control over his power from earlier long gone and showing how pissed off he was. Colors flew away from him in every direction as he shouted, "You fucking crazy person!"

"What if I told you the written portion was a lie," You said with a shrug, unconcerned and very much, just, *you*, "Though I wish it wasn't."

"How would that help!" Nolan exploded, emotionally and literally. I cringed as I was mildly blinded, blinking spots out of my eyes.

"I don't know, I'm kinda happy about not having to do another test," Chase said, and Nolan reeled around to glare at him, but Chase just shrugged in response, "What? At least nobody died."

"Wow, such a low bar," Warren rolled his eyes, lips turned up in a scowl.

"Wait a second. . .I just realized you used your phone at the beginning!" I yelled as if that was the point I really, really needed to get across, "Mrs. Briar never even turned off anything!"

"Nope," Oliver said, and he looked like he was trying hard not to laugh, "There was gas in the boats the whole time too."

I can't believe this.

I really can't!

I put my head in my hands, "We were duped. So. Hard."

Kalei stepped forward, her expression stern, "Even if this was just a test, the other students could have gotten hurt. What about them, huh?"

"Oh," Tristan and Anna said at the same time, which was hella freaky, "Don't worry about that."

"Should I break it to them?" Oliver asked, "I do have a kinder face."

"Oh, what now!?" Nolan yelled, and all the teachers shared a conspiratorial glance, "Why are you looking at each other like that? Tell us!"

"Uh, haha," Oliver laughed awkwardly, "We're just trying to figure out how to say it gently. . ."

"Just say it bluntly then." Warren said, his arms crossed and tapping his foot against the cement aggressively, "I doubt it could get worse."

Oliver grimaced, and that was not a good sign for what was to come. He looked back at the other teachers, and they made the go-on gesture, and he sighed, "Okay, blunt it is then. . ."

Oliver clasped his hand together as if he was apologizing or saying a prayer, "We've been lying to you the whole time."

"No, duh?" Adya said gruffly, "That didn't explain shit."

"Not all of it!" Oliver quickly amended when he saw the looks of pure sass on our faces, "You are here to become vigilantes, I swear!"

"Okay, what have you lied about?" Ryuma spoke up from the back, and he seemed more genuinely curious than angry. The lone outlier in the mass of aggravation that surrounded him.

"I thought you were going to be blunt," You said with a sign as you hopped off the stage. You walked up to stand next to Oliver and told it to us straight:

"Everyone at this school is training to be vigilantes, not just you."

What.

The.

Hell?

What the hell was that supposed to mean!?

"Your class is different, though!" Triston continued in our stunned silence, "I wasn't lying when I said we chose you guys from a lottery. We scouted the rest of the classes for their abilities, but we decided to try something different this year. To see if we could give kids without powers, uh, powers?"

"And don't get a big head about you managing to keep the 'secret.' The other classes knew the whole time. We do this exercise every year. You'll get to experience the joy of watching next year's class fumble around trying to hide their powers from everyone. It's the highlight of the year, in my opinion."

"So you're saying," Will said from where he was leaning heavily on Micah's shoulder, "That Freedom bay high school has always been a school for vigilantes?"

"Yep!"

"And we've been trying to keep our powers a secret even though everyone else has powers too?"

"Bingo!"

"And this was our semester exam?" Will said tiredly, and Micah gave him a concerned look, holding onto him tighter.

"Yes! And no." Triton said, "There is one more thing we have to tell you. This party isn't just for you completing your exam."

"Um, so there's. . .more?" Jason said warily. Harley was still in his grip, but I think it was more to keep Jason stable than to protect Harley. Harley had been nodding along the whole time. . . Did he really figure all of this out?

I wouldn't be surprised, honestly.

"It's also a celebration of you debuting as vigilantes!" Triston said proudly, "Isn't that great?"

"Wait, you mean-" I said as all the dots aligned to draw a picture of you smirking in my head.

"Everything you kids just did was recorded," Oliver said, almost remorseful as he pulled out his cell. He thumbed through his phone then turned it to face us. On the screen was a live broadcast of a Hawaiian news station:

"-We have new insight on the breaking story of the superhero attack at Freedom Bay Highschool. A group of vigilantes arrived on the scene in time to rescue the students and staff from the intruders. The motive is still unclear-"

"It's all over social media too," You said nonchalantly, "A few of your upperclassmen volunteered to post your brave deeds."

"Oh my god." I breathed out.

Because, really, *oh my god.*

"So, now that's out of the way," Tristan said cheekily as if the conversion we were just having wasn't completely and utterly mind-blowing. As if maybe we would like to, I don't know, take a breath at some point before we all inevitably lose our minds?

Nope, we get none of that because he just says:

"Let's eat."

And that's how my class passed our exams, found out that everything we were told was a complete lie, and debuted as vigilantes on the same night.

At least the pizza was good, I guess. . .

☁ Chapter 13 ☁

In summary, here are all the questions (and answers) we had asked that night (in no apparent order):

Q: Wait, so you had this party set up from the beginning?
A: Nope! We had to move everything with the help of the senior class to the secret fountain room because Harley figured out what was going on early. ("Oops?" Harley blushed as he chomped on his pizza.)

Q: (To Oliver) But you were bleeding!?
A: It was just fake blood, hahaha! Don't worry! (looked real to me, ass.)

Q: But isn't your wife going to be on the news as a villain? Isn't that bad?

A: We haven't sent the footage yet. We just told them that we had to go through the proper channels before the public could see it. We also told them the footage was a bit corrupted, so we couldn't get a good image of the superheroes. We'll give them the edited version later.

Q: How did you set this all up so the news station knew so fast?

A: I know a guy. (You never explained this, and I'm kinda irritated about that.)

Q: What if we hurt someone?

A: Hun, there were literally over a hundred people that could have stopped you. Plus, no one was actually tied up, so they could have avoided you.

Q: How are people going to know what our vigilante names are? We never said them.

A: The power of editing and stellar journalism.

Q: Doesn't this look bad for the school?

A: Nah, it'll be fine! If anything, we might get pity points and extra donations.

Q: Who cooked this pizza? It's the best thing I've tasted in my *life.*

A: Brad. He used to work at a pizza parlor back in the day. Yum!

Q: But. . .the acting was way too good! Like, you seemed shocked, terrified, etcetera!

A: If you want to be a vigilante, you have to master lying. Secret identities, cover stories, there's a lot of lying to be had in this line of work. (I just realized that our first encounter makes soooooo much more sense now.)

Q: Who are Jose and Angela?

A: *shrug* I don't know, I just made them up. (. . . I have no words, omg.)

Q: So did we do a good job hiding our powers, or were the other classes pretending not to see?

A: Of course they were pretending! That's part of their curriculum, you know. They hide from you as much as you hide from them; you'll get better at it! But I gotta say, I think the moment that people latched onto the most was the water monster incident. Micah pushing Jason back into the ocean was funny for *weeks.*

*****

I couldn't stop staring at my phone for the whole flight back home for winter break.

I was bombarded with news alerts, social media posts, and texts from my classmates. It was surreal that the day before, I had debuted as a Vigilante, and now people knew my secret identity. Like, I'm still shook that someone edited my debut into a meme. A very catchy meme that remixed my 'Evildoer, I have come to stop you!' line into a bop of a song, and I didn't know whether to feel like I needed to die from embarrassment or be oddly touched.

(I still come back to that video every once and a while. Did you know it surpassed 10 million views last week?. .(0_0). . .)

It's crazy to think about how Triston managed to pull everything off with his various connections. Making sure that our real identities, including his wife, remained a secret through extensive editing and distractionary tactics. He said he had to put a lot of thought into this plan because he's never debuted so many people at once, let alone a first-year class. It usually was consistently spaced out, one or two students at a time and in different parts of the world. It made me think of the news reports that said that Vigilante debuts have been on the rise for about a decade. With a quick google search, the growth started a few years after Freedom bay high school was first built. . .

Coincidence? I think not!

But I knew that because I was aware of the secret, I could read between the lines. Triston was so good at hiding his tracks that nobody could connect that most of the vigilantes from this era were secretly trained at his school. Almost all of the vigilantes I adored were my school's alumni, and that's. . .crazy with a capital 'C.'

It's also freaking mind-blowing that even the *government* doesn't know what Triston has been sneakily doing for years. Like, What!? How!? When I asked him about it, only moments before I got on the boat of doom, he smiled and said, "Sometimes brainwashing can be used for the sake of good."

My jaw had dropped, and Triston laughed as he pushed me the final few steps off the dock and into my ride to the mainland.

Bonkers.

Just utterly bonkers what I've gotten myself into.

When I finally got off the plane, my family greeted me (plus Alex and his mom's), and it wasn't long before Mom ran over and pulled me into a bone-crushing hug, "Sky, I'm glad you're okay!"

"Mom, I'm fine." I said, strained because of the lack of air entering my lungs, "I texted you last night. . .Mom. . . seriously can't breathe. . ."

"Oops!" Mom said as she hurriedly got rid of the pressure. Her hands moved up to loosely land on my shoulders instead, "Sorry, sorry. I just worry. There have been so many attacks lately. . .and for it to be at your school. . ."

"I know," I smile at her, but she doesn't loosen her grip just yet, "Really, I'm fine. It wasn't even that scary."

"Are you sure?" Mom peered across my face, searching, "Do we need to take you to see someone? Are you hurt? Did they do anything to you? Oh, gosh!"

"Mom!" I yelled out in exasperation, and a few heads turned our way in curiosity. I leaned in and whispered, "I'm fine! I didn't even get a scratch!"

My mom gave me the 'look.' You know the look when your mom really, really cares about your wellbeing but is trying to be chill? That look.

I let out a small sigh and gave my mom a gentle smile, "I'm fine. I promise."

She looked like she wanted to say more, but at that moment, Alex couldn't hold it in anymore, his words bubbling out, "So what was it like to see vigilantes in action? I bet it was *awesome!*"

"Oh, yeah, it was so cool, like being in an action movie," I said excitedly even though I was technically the action star in this metaphorical film. But Alex didn't need to know that, though.

Rule #1: Learn to lie.

Alex beamed at me, bigger and broader than I've ever seen, "You're going to have to *tell me all about it.*"

My mom let you a tired but fond sigh, "Alright. Alright. . .let's get you home."

*****

That night I had another party.

It was a mix of a coming home party and, as Alex dubbed it before his mom, Laura whacked his shoulder, a 'you're not dead!' party. The house was decorated for Christmas, the tree tucked in the corner, and winter-themed lights, streamers, and knickknacks scattered around. Our family always had the tradition of making the decorations as unappealing to look at as possible. It all started when I was a kid, and I knocked into the tree and broke the top clean off. We had to tape it back on. After that, decorations would be hung up wrong, little snowmen would be laid on their side as if our cat had knocked it over, and we would always break off the top of the tree to memorialize that fateful day.

Chaos was the Hayes family's greatest pastime.

I had just shoved one of Bethany's famous cookies in my mouth when Alex tapped my shoulder, "Hey, as much as I love to watch your dad struggle playing twister-."

"I'm. . .not. . .struggling!" My dad huffed as he tried to reach for a red dot, weaving his arm through my mom's elevated back, "I'm the king of Twister!"

"Uh-huh, keep telling yourself that, Dad," Jamie said with a roll of her eyes, leaning against the kitchen counter, "Don't come to me if you break your back."

"I'm not that old! I'm thirty-six!" My dad yelled, scandalized. His hand slipped, and he fell forward into my mom, and both of them crashed to the floor in a pile of limbs, "Oof!"

Bethany let out a laugh from the gut, so loud it was always shocking that it could come out of her petite frame. She leaned forward, her chuckles shaking her enough that her dirty blonde hair came slightly loose from her bun. Laura gave her wife a fond smile, her green eyes shining in pure love, and said, "Maybe we should play Monopoly instead?"

"Oh no!" Alex bellowed, jumping to his feet and grabbing my arm, "I will not partake in that kind of torture! Hurry, let's get out of here!"

Alex yanked on my arm, and I almost sprawled to the floor as he dragged me out of the living room and into the hallway. He sprinted us upstairs and quickly shut my bedroom door to the sound of Bethany's hearty laughter. He turned to me, his back pressed against my door.

"What happened in the last game of monopoly?" I asked, but Alex just gave me a long, hard stare.

Then without breaking eye contact, he reached up to the doorknob and turned the lock in place with a click, "We need to talk."

"Uhhh," I said, mildly terrified. That was Alex's serious face, and I ran through our last interactions to figure out what I did to get the 'stare.' Had I somehow offended him through one of my texts? I scanned my memory to double, triple check but came up empty.

Alex marched over after I looked through the past six months as if it was a flipbook and slapped his hands onto my shoulders, "We're best friends, right?"

I blinked in confusion, pages coming to a halt in my head, "What? Of course, you are!"

Alex pursed his lips and raised an eyebrow, leaning in, "You know that I still remember the time you stole that snickers bar when we were six?"

Okay, now I DEFINITELY didn't know where the heck this conversion was going, "Huh?"

Alex let out an exasperated sigh and fell back onto my bed, "So you're not going to tell me?"

"Tell you what?"

"C'mon, Sky."

"What the hell are you *talking about?*" I asked as I got the sudden urge to pull at his cheeks in frustration.

"Fine, be that way," Alex said with an exaggerated huff, "I'm *talking about* how you're SkyRocket. Duh!"

My mind's gears exploded, all smoke and dust and springs flying out my ears. First, I was too shocked to think about anything, but then all my thoughts rushed through my mind at the speed of a bullet train. Wait, What Did He Just Say? OMGdidhejustsaywhatIthoughthejustsaid? But How Did He Make The Connection! Ohfudgeimafailureatbeingaviglante! Omg! Howdoitellhimit'salie . . .But It's Not Though! Ahhhhhhhhhhhh! Red Alert! WEE WOO, WEE WOO! HELP!!

My thoughts must have shown on my face because Alex's expression softened, and he waved a hand in a placating gesture, "C'mon, man. It wasn't that hard to figure out. I've known you since we were like five. Hell, your vigilante name has your *real* name in it. A dead Skylar giveaway to make your name a pun."

"But the video modified my voice! And you couldn't see my face! And-," I pause as the realization of what I just said takes hold, "Shit, I just admitted it didn't I?"

I slapped my forehead, partly punishing myself for my dumb idiot mistake of breaking Rule #1 so fast.

"Yes, you just did," Alex said as his lips twitched as he tried to hold in his laughter, "But don't worry, I don't think anyone else has figured it out yet."

I flopped into my desk chair and titled my head to stare at the ceiling. After a hearty pause, I just had to say, "So. You figured it out?"

"Yep."

"But how though?"

Alex seemed to think about his answer, eyeing me sideways from my own bed, "Like I said, I know you. Plus, the evidence lines up if you're looking for it. The attack on the school, the number of vigilantes being the same amount of kids from your class, the pun name... But the thing that gave you away was that you didn't text me immediately with the daring rescue details. C'mon Sky, you and I both know we're vigilante fanboys."

"Wha-," I try to protest, but then I rapidly click my mouth shut before saying feebly, "Okay, you got a point."

"Don't I, though? Now. . ." Alex leaned forward, his smile growing wide, "Give me all the juicy details of Who's who? What exactly haven't you told me yet? And-" Alex paused before pointing at me, ". . . also if you want to keep your secret, maybe don't do *that*."

I blinked and then fell the few feet I levitated back into my chair, the force causing me to wreck and crash to the floor, the chair going one way and my body going the other.

And no matter what I said for the next few minutes, Alex wouldn't stop laughing.

So, yeah. That's how I found out my best friend knew of my secret identity. And, I guess, that he was way more observant than I ever gave him credit for...

But to be honest, I was relieved. As much as I thought being a vigilante would be awesome and embraced it with open arms, it was sad to think...

that I would have to keep this heavy burden of the secret from my friends and family.

And as I explained to Alex my school adventures, about my class and our powers, it was nice to get it off my chest. I knew I needed to 'learn to lie' so I could keep the people I love safe, but it was nice to have someone to confide in. That ONE person that I could talk to from my previous life before everything got mind-boggling crazy. Before the powers, before I couldn't be genuinely truthful with anyone.

As for keeping the secret to himself, I knew Alex would take our secret to his grave.

Our friendship was too solid for him to do anything else.

(Though I did have to promise to keep him up to date, or he would make sure there would be no more Bethany cookies. PURE EVIL, I TELL YOU!)

I don't know why I have to tell you about how Alex can keep a secret. You know first-hand soooooooooo:

Yeah, moving on.

*****

You know this is the first time I don't want to write what happens next. Sure, I'm still a little salty about writing this to begin with, but. . .the only thing that I think I HAVE to mention before moving on from first year was, you know, *that incident.* Other than *the incident,* nothing too important happens to us, considering you wanted us to keep on the down-low for a while before getting back to vigilante duties in public. Also, the fact that our class doesn't interact with the other classes until our second year, so our training is the basic 'getting better at our powers' shtick.

. . .I'm just going to have to suck it up and get through this, I guess. But I also feel like I need to explain how it got to *that incident* and that I wasn't a total idiot for not seeing it coming. . .

Sigh.

Fine.

Here we go:

Going back to class in January was a weird experience now that none of the classes had to pretend anymore. It was like the school flipped a switch, and suddenly everyone was using powers for absolutely anything. Late for class? Powers. Don't want to carry your books? Powers. Want to surprise someone? Powers. Homework? Powers.

Anything? Powers.

The halls were a frenzy of activity as I rushed to class. One guy slipped into the shadows next to me and disappeared. A girl yelled at me to watch out as she sailed past me, sliding against the ground with no shoes as if her feet were skates. Another guy let out sparkes from his hair, his face firetruck red as a pretty girl asked him how his break was. Another person threw a water bottle over my head, and his friend from across the hall snatched it from the air with a hand that grew 20 times bigger before shrinking back to average size.

It's incredible to think that these same kids were just ordinary students in my eyes only a few weeks ago. And that I never noticed any of them slip up and use their powers in front of me...

It made me feel like I had a lot to learn.

I slid into my seat just as the bell rang, "I kind of feel like I have whiplash."

"I know," Jason said, his eyes a little wider than usual. Probably still a bit in shock. He leaned forward to whisper, "Apparently, some of them have been using the fountain to get to training without us realizing..."

"What? But how!?" I said, my brain was just a thought bubble saying '!?!?!?!?!'.

Jason shrugged helplessly, "Seniors?"

I didn't know what to say to that, but luckily I didn't have to because you opened the door and lazily strolled in front of the whiteboard, "I would ask how your breaks were, but I don't care."

"Oh! Did that pretty lady go on that date with you?" Harley asked innocently, and Chase's hand flew to his mouth, unsuccessfully covering up his snort. Your face froze as if it didn't remember how to show emotion correctly.

"That bad?" Jake asked in a mock gentle voice, "I'm so sorry for your loss. . ."

"SO-"

"Nice deflection, teach." Surprisingly Adya teased, and I choked on my laughter. Like, seriously, I almost died; thanks a lot, Adya.

"SO," You continued again, full-on ignoring Jake's comment and Harley's question, and Adya's disrespect (and my death), "We are doing a school-wide event this week."

It might have been my imagination, but I think everyone sat up a little straighter in interest. Yes, even Ethan and Nolan. I think everyone went down the same train of thought: if this event has every class AFTER the big reveal, that would mean-!?

"Is it a competition!? Class v.s. class in a fight of strength and awesomeness?" Chase blurted in excitement, "It has to be, right? C'mon teach, don't leave us hanging!"

You blinked and let out a loud snort until your laugh grew so loud it echoed around the room. As your gasps grew more manic, everyone slowly deflated until all we were doing was waiting to be disappointed. Or worse. . .waiting for the threat of training.

Finally, *finally,* you straightened up, "Okay, that was genuinely funny. I haven't laughed so hard in years. They would kick your ass, hahaha!"

You turned around, shoulder's still shaking, and reached for a black dry erase marker and started to write, "The event is our school's annual beach clean-up, pfft. Haha, phew, okay, haha, alright! Everyone will be split into groups of three and get a section of beach to comb over."

You cleared your throat to dislodge the last as your laughter, turning back around to face us, "It's our way to give back to the community."

"Oh," Micah said, almost sounding relieved, "Well, that's anticlimactic. . ."

"You want me to make it more climactic for you?" You said, raising a skeptical eyebrow.

"NO!"

☁ Chapter 14 ☁

We all agreed to draw lots to see who would be in each group. It only seemed fair. Plus, we didn't want to risk YOU making the groups because I know for a fact you would have been a total jerk about it. Better to leave it to chance than leave it to you. My group was with the twins. And I think that was truly the start of my misfortune. Honestly, you could even say that maybe it's the twin's fault that led to *that incident.* I mean technically. . .

I'm stalling. I'm so stalling. . .

UGH.

Fine.

After we crossed the water on the boats, our class stuffed ourselves into a bus, and we were carted to one of the beaches that Triston signed on for us to clean. We went to one of the more popular destinations on the island. Hence, we had to weave through families on vacation and locals sunbathing. I wondered at the time if Triston chose the more populated beach for us so we could try not to 'pop off' powers-wise. Was this secretly training mixed with the helping hand of community service?

Triston did say something about how being a vigilante isn't all about fighting cool battles and helping out in other ways, so maybe?

Anyway, we were picking up trash when:

"*Ptew!* Seriously guys? Can you not be the stereotypical twin characters for five minutes," I said as I spit out a glob of sand, the grains gritty against my teeth. For almost the whole time we were on the beach, the twins had made a game out of the trip and were tossing the trash into each other's bags, laughing and getting sand everywhere.

An old lady gave us the stink eye, and I thought, 'Is it bad that I kinda want to be a fourth wheel with the Adya-Harley-Ryuma group?' No, past me, it's not. Anything to do with Harley is a blessing.

"Aww, C'mon Sky, *live* a little," Jake said cheekily before Chase reached down, cupped some water in his hand, and hurled it at his brother. In retaliation, Jake kicked out and did a sweeping slash of water, his sandal flying away in his assault. The shoe flew twenty feet until it hit the top of someone's beach umbrella, bounced off, and sailed across the beach until it landed right next to that old lady from before.

If looks could kill, that old lady would have instantly turned us to dust.

Which was valid, in all honesty.

But that didn't stop me from finally caving, and I laughed so hard that I couldn't see through the tears. It was always a losing battle, and I was proud I lasted as long as I did. Then, as Jake made the walk of shame to retrieve his shoe, apologizing to the irate woman, I used my trash grabber and flicked out into the water to soak Chase.

"Oh, you don't know what you just started. That water war has begun!" Chase yelled, tossing his trash bag and grabber to the side before full-on tackling me into the water. I skidded on my back until we were almost submerged in the waves.

I scrambled to my feet. As Chase said: the ultimate water war had begun, and there was no turning back. My honor was on the line. I lunged forward and put my arms around Chase's waist, and hoisted him up. And with a bit of help from my power, I chucked him deeper into the waves, watching with a smug look as he was fully submerged, "Ha, ha! Take that!"

And then that was when Layla came shooting in like a rogue mercenary and pushed me down with a cackle. She, like a coward, zipped away back to her group (Her, Nolan, and Warren) before I could get her back. When I came up for air, flinging my hair out of my eyes, I saw Warren pinching the bridge of his nose and Nolan clutching his grabber so hard his knuckles were white. When we made eye contact, he huffed and strutted away, kicking up sand.

"Alright, alright! Settle down!" Oliver said, walking towards us with you ambling behind him. It's funny. I knew that with that twinkle in his eye, he wanted to turn around and push you into the water just as much as I want to right now. Metaphorically, of course. . .Yeah, you know what? He would totally push you in if he wasn't the classy one in this situation.

Soon, The Great Water war ended with a mutual cease-fire, negotiated by a neutral foreign power. I reached behind me to help Chase up, "Truce?"

Chase just grinned and grasped my hand so fast that it was almost suspicious. I was halfway pulling him up when someone tapped my shoulder. Chase's lips folded in on themselves as his expression became impish, "Opp."

Suspicious.

"Yeah?" I asked as I turned around, half expecting to get whacked in the head with Jake's sandal by that old lady. But, instead, I was face to face with a pretty girl my age. She was wearing an orangish-pink bikini, and her long black hair was pulled up into a messy bun. Her brown eyes sparkled, and her smile was timid but also somehow confident. She had a necklace strung around her neck, two colorful beads surrounding a vibrant green gem.

I was very conscious of how my clothes were sticking to my body from all the water, "Uh, hi? Do you need something?"

I was *also* very conscious of Jake, Chase, Layla, Warren, Oliver and you staring at me as the interaction unfolded. Even Nolan was side-eyeing me a little bit away, trying to subtly pick up a piece of trash with little success. Oh, and VERY aware of Chase poking into my back repeatedly. Which wasn't helping, you gremlin! Stop!

The mysterious girl reached up to fiddle with her necklace, "Um, I was wondering. . ."

My brain was starting to realize exactly what was happening, and my cheeks heated to the point you could probably see my blush from space. Warren quickly looked away and grabbed Layla, dragging her away as she yelped out, "Aww, it was just getting good!"

The girl was unfazed, or at least she pretended to be a good sport about my embarrassing friends, "I was wondering if maybe you would like to exchange numbers?"

And that's when my brain fully imploded. I froze, my eyes wide, and Oliver bit his lip to hold in his laughter. However, you had no qualms and burst out laughing, waving to me as you walked away, "Good luck with that!"

Chase grabbed my shoulders from behind and shook me slightly, probably making me look like a bobblehead, "Dude, what are you doing! Answer her!"

For her part, the girl was just smiling, and I blurted out, "Sure!"

She clapped her hand excitedly, "Cool! Um, um, hold on just a second, I'll be right back!"

She jogged off, and I whispered, "What just happened?"

"I think that this is what you kids call 'getting asked out'?" Oliver said with air quotes and a faux sense of seriousness that did nothing to mask his mouth twitching in suppressed laughter.

"Way to go, dude!" Chase yelled excitedly, "Way to get the girl!"

"But I didn't do anything?" I asked, still a bit shocked that I really HAD just been asked out on a date.

"Maybe she likes awkward. I don't know, man," Chase said with a shrug, and I was a little offended.

Before I could express my hurt, the girl came back, her cellphone in hand, "Can I have your number? I'll text you."

"Ah, YES!" I said and internally cringed. She laughed, and I gave her my number, embarrassed. Once done, she looked up into my eyes, "And your name, you know, for the contact?"

"Skylar."

"Sky. . .lar. Okay, cool name!" She said as she shoved her phone into the top of her bikini, a part of it sticking out the side. She smiled, "Tamara, by the way. Tamara Douglas, that's my, uh, name."

We stared at each other for maybe too long before she straightened up, "Okay, anyway, bye! I'll text you!"

She walked away with a wave and disappeared into the crowd.

And that was the start.

The beginning of *that incident.*

*****

Tamara texted me that night, all exclamation points and smiley faces. I could barely focus on the English homework I was trying to help Nolan with, my phone buzzing every few seconds. It got to the point that Nolan scowled and just left the dorm with an 'oh, fuck this' and a slam of the door, the light above the door flickering from the impact.

I decided I'd help him later and put my full attention to my replies. Tamara and I had a lot in common. We liked the same shows, the same music, and were the same kind of awkward, so we bounced off each other well. She lived in Hawaii all her life, and even though the sun and sand were great and all, she wanted to see more of the world than her tiny cluster of islands.

We chatted into the night, and I admit that I had a lot of fun talking to her. But there was one crucial detail that she hadn't entirely made clear until a few days later:

She just wanted to be friends.

Which, cool.

That's fine.

. . .I was only a little devastated.

*****

As the months flew by, many instances stood out to me, both with school and Tamara Douglas.

Let's start with school because as much as I would *love* to write about *that incident,* we did a few things that I have to include. What's the point of this assignment if I didn't, right?

Even though we weren't going to train with any of the upper classes until sophomore year, training was still intense. And since we did have basic control of our powers, we also squeezed in more effective combat lessons into every class of Vigilante Studies.

Gone were the reckless jabs and grabs from our final exam, and in their place was a more practiced approach. You even went through the effort to show us moves that would fit our fighting styles, keeping our powers and weaknesses in mind. I don't think I've ever worked out that hard before coming to this school, but it was paying off. I gained a fair bit of muscle, and I could hold my own in sparring matches.

Unless it was with Adya.

I'm always going to be afraid of Adya.

Power-wise I was able to move larger objects and more at once. It still took a lot of concentration, but I could also lift a person without touching them. (Harley had the best time floating above me as I navigated the obstacle course, talking to his bird friend Louise.)

So, all in all, I was getting stronger...

Now for Tamara.

We kept in touch and hung out together often. Sure my heart was a little broken from being shoved brutally into the friend zone, but I did like talking to her. And after a while, the sting faded, and I was able to just enjoy her company...

But hindsight's 20/20, and now all I can think about were the little hints she had sprinkled in. Little snippets of her true intentions as the mouths drew on, warning signs that I failed to see...

Like the first time, she and I went into town. We had just finished up a round of laser tag when she had offhandedly said, "You know, when I first saw you, I swore I'd seen you somewhere before. Weird, huh?"

Or another time, when we had milkshakes by the beach on a particularly sweltering day, she mentioned that she was fascinated with the history of Superheroes. Like how crazy it was for one guy to change the world like that. That they could be so powerful...

And...what she said a week before *the incident:* "Man, wouldn't it be pretty cool if I could fly?

Just leave this island for good. Like, I'm so jealous of that new vigilante!"

But at the same time, all of the hints were drowned out by everything else we talked about, how much fun we had. So my mind washed away the warnings, down the river of regret.

I can't stall anymore, dammit.

Time to write about THE incident.

*****

It happened in the final week of the school year. Tamara and I were walking in town, and the sky had fully darkened around us so that the only source of light was coming from the street lamps. I had just texted Nolan an answer to a question he was having trouble with, glanced at the time, and put my phone in my pocket, "Well, I better get going."

"Aww, lame," Tamara said with a pout, fiddling with her necklace, "I just wanted to show you something too!"

That piqued my interest, "What is it?"

"A secret hideout," She said mischievously, raising her hands and wiggling her fingers dramatically.

I pretended like I hadn't already decided that I was going to see this secret hideout, "Hideout, you say...well, I guess a slight detour won't kill anyone..."

"Yes," Tamara pumped her fist in the air, and I laughed at her enthusiasm. Then, she reached forward and grabbed my wrist, "I'll take you then! Secret hideout, ho!"

And with her hand gripping my wrist, she ran us down side streets, across a busy intersection despite the late hour, and over a chain-link fence. Dropping down onto beat-up concrete with weeds growing the cracks, I looked at our destination, "An old mall?"

"Yep," Tamara said as she walked toward the side entrance, pulling her hair into a ponytail as she went, "The mall shut down over twenty years ago, and the city doesn't have the money to tear it down. Perfect place for a secret hideout, don't you think?."

"Are you sure we won't get into trouble for trespassing?" I asked as she reached out and pulled the glass door open, the lock looking like it had broken a long time ago.

Tamara rolled her eyes, "No, we won't get in trouble. Now come over here before I leave you outside."

I hustled to stand beside her, and she closed the door behind me. The hallway was dark, but I made out signs for restrooms on one side due to the small amount of light coming from the end of the hall. Tamara pulled out her phone and turned on the flashlight. The beam went down the hallway and confirmed my assessment that this hallway was just for the public restrooms.

"We just have to round the corner, and we'll be able to see better. There's a giant skylight." Tamara said with a shrug and went on ahead. I followed her, and she put her phone away as we got closer; after we exited the hallway with the restrooms and passed a few boarded-up stores. Ahead of us was a large open area where the skylight was, light from the moon shining down into the middle of the mall.

I walked out into the open space, "Man, it's kinda creepy, isn't it?"

Tamara's voice was far away as I heard her run off, "Yeah, I guess I kind of is! Give me a second, and I'll turn on the overhead lights!"

"Uh, maybe we shouldn't? It might tell people were here." I said as I turned to look for her, but she was gone. I sighed and sat down on the fountain's ledge, the water inside still there but murky and discolored. I waited there for a while and wondered how long it would take her to turn on the lights.

Yes, I'm a fucking idiot for not seeing where this was going.

Okay?

I get it!

"Tamara?" I yelled, and that's when it happened.

"I'm here," I heard her shout, and luckily I turned toward the voice just in time to see a large piece of concrete come flying straight at my head. I dodged in time, but the hardened rock grazed me, and I felt a slight trickle of blood start to run down my cheek.

And there was Tamara, on the second floor, pieces of the building gliding around her body, twisting around along with the movement of her fingers. And the thing that still gets me to this day was that her smile wasn't crazed. It wasn't like a villain at all.

It was Tamara's usual smile.

"You have powers?" I exclaimed in shock before my brain realized what I should be asking, "What the hell are you doing!?"

"Are you going to fly?" Tamara asked, tilting her head.

"What?"

"Are you going to fly, SkyRocket?" Tamara asked naturally as if we were chilling like usual, drinking shakes and dipping our fries, "Because if you don't, I'm going to kill you."

I froze, and she saw my moment of weakness for what it was and hurled another ball of concrete at me. Again, I barely dodged, losing my balance and falling to the floor. I had to roll to get away from the next attack, "Even if I was him, why are you attacking me!?"

"Because," Tamara said with an expression as light as air, "I saw you fly at the beach that day when you threw your friend. You have to be a part of that group that saved that rich kid's school."

"But, I'm not-"

She continued as if me trying to make excuses bored her, "No, you are. It's oblivious at this point. I hoped by befriending you, you might let something slip, but I can't wait anymore. You're going to tell me what I want, and I'm going to get rid of you. One less vigilante to deal with."

"You're a Super," I said in one reluctant breath.

"Yep! It's funny," Tamara said as she leaned against the railing, posture relaxed, "Being born into a family of superheroes tends to send you down that path. A self-fulfilling prophecy. . .but, I'm done talking."

She reached out her left hand and clenched her fist. The wall next to her cracked, then broke away, flying in to refill her ammo, "Tell me who the other vigilantes are, and I'll make your death quick."

🌣 Chapter 15 🌣

"What a cliche line!" I yelled as I dove into the nearest shop, bits of drywall dusting my hair and shards of glass flying over my head, "The whole monologue thing is so last century!"

Even though I was trying to act cool on the outside, inside, I was a blubbering mess of confusion, panic, and altogether just 'AHHHHHHHHHHHI!!!!!!! Holy shit!" Like how would you react if the girl you kind of didn't fully get over but still wanted to be friends with started hurling drywall, cement, and glass at you? As she's flying on the part of the ground she herself had ripped up? And that she was trying to take me out. Full-on no more Skylar, six-feet under, superhero murder? ~~Also, is it weird that I was a little bit more attracted to Tamara at that moment? . . . Do I have a type? ALSO, why the hell did I just write that! To YOU. Fuuck.~~

It was like I was in a plothole-filled action movie where the film is already showing the villain, and we still got 50 more minutes left to watch the main character contemplate their life choices. Like I'm contemplating if this assignment is worth the effort right now. If my utter embarrassment doesn't want me to crawl under a rock and DIE.

I dove behind the counter where a rundown cash register was, and just in time too as Tamara crashed through the front of the store, sending discarded shelving and racks skidding across the aged carpet. She was hovering a few feet off the ground, her ponytail a hurricane around her head, the curls whipping around like medusa's snakes. One hand was faced down to control her crude hovercraft, and the other near her shoulder, her fingers twirling along with the bits of the mall she had amassed.

She paused, and her hair settled on her black graphic t-shirt, covering up part of the design, "Skylar, come on. Stop running."

I wasn't going to fall for her petty trick to lure me out. . .no SIR.

"Like hell!" I shouted like the complete fool I was, and her eyes jerked to the counter, and she threw out her left arm like a softball pitch. The counter, register, and the wall were pelted like an intense hail storm, the debris hitting so hard that they went straight through like bullets. I flinched and threw up my arms to cover my head. With the movement, my power kicked in, mostly survival instinct than me trying to use it, and I stopped her attack from hitting me.

I stared at the floating pieces and then, very heroic like, jumped out of my hiding place, sweeping my arm out like a magician showing off his next trick, "Catch!"

Tamara snarled as her ammunition sailed back at her. I took the small moment of hesitation and fled, jumping through the ruined window and cutting my legs. I sprinted to the main exit, my shadow trailing behind me in the light of the moon, and just barely reached the sliding doors when Tamara shouted, "You think you can get away!"

The ground under me shook, and I stumbled forward. My head smacked against the glass of the doors, making me bite my tongue. Blood filled my mouth, and then I was in the air. Flung backward from the earth as if I had a rug pulled out from under me. I fell onto my back against the linoleum flooring.

I groaned as I pushed myself up, "Not making this easy, are you?"

I couldn't see Tamara rolling her eyes, but I could *feel* it, "Just tell me who you're working with already."

"I could do that," I said as I lifted myself to my full height. Posturing as if I had the upper hand in this battle of wills, "Or I could just beat you and turn you in!"

Tamara scoffed, loud and echoing off the walls. Her eyes shined with annoyance in the white light of the moon, "Really? *Really?* Do you think you can win? Look at you! I haven't even been trying!"

Despite the situation, I paused, "Wait, are you serious?"

"Ugh," Tamara groaned, "Vigilantes are getting worse by the generation."

"We're the same age!"

"No offense Skylar but you have the maturity of a five-year-old," Tamara said, and I took all of the offense, "Just tell me what I want to know, and maybe I'll let you live."

"See, that right there is another cliche line that no one would agree to!" I said, bracing myself for her inevitable retaliation.

And. . .Tamara was done talking. She closed her eyes for a moment as if to pray for my death. Then, taking a deep breath, her eyes snapped open, and her mouth formed into a sneer. I jumped into the air the moment she chucked another boulder at me, barely missing my legs. I went straight up as if I was that thing that zooms to the top of those test your strength carnival games. So fast that I almost rammed directly into the ceiling.

With a yelp, I stopped myself and flipped over, so my back was against the skylight. Looking down, I saw Tamara slap her hand against the fountain. I pushed off with all the strength in my legs as the uprooted fountain shot up to meet me. I ungracefully flopped onto the second floor as the fountain continued on its course, smashing through the glass and steel connecting beams and into the dark.

That's when I noticed that it had started to rain, the beads of water descending into the mall without the barrier to stop it, hitting the floor with sharp splats. I peered down for only a second to see Tamara looking right back at me, her skin now wet and her hair sticking to her forehead.

Then I got the hell out of there.

Sprinting closer to the storefronts, I only made it past a few locked up stores before Tamara appeared beside me, again on her hover surfboard of death. She reached out with her free hand, and the floor in front of me crumbled upwards before sailing straight towards me. I backpedaled, and my shoes skidded across the ground with a loud squeak as I changed direction and leaped across the opening between the balconies of the second floor. I missed Tamara by inches as she continued flying forward, her hair smacking me in the face.

Before she could turn around, I dove into another store, this time going a bit farther and into the back room. I flicked my wrist and prayed that my power would listen and give me some slack. All the furniture moved to barricade the door. It wasn't going to hold long, and I knew it wouldn't. So instead, I did what any good vigilante in a pickle would do:

I called for backup.

My fingers shook as I fumbled for my phone, and in my head, I knew I couldn't call the police because, uh, secret identity? So in my panic, I called the first person in my recent contacts. The phone rang three agonizing times before it stopped mid-ring on the fourth.

I didn't wait for the person to say hello, frantically spouting, "Help! I'm in an abandoned mall, and Tamara is trying to kill me!"

There was a long pause before the person on the other end laughed. And I mean, busting a gut, wheezing, and snorting laughter. And that's when I realized who I had just called for help. My mind flashed back to who I had texted about twenty minutes ago about English homework...

"Oh, fuck yes, this is beautiful," Nolan-fucking-Edwards said with delight.

"Nolan, this is serious!" I hissed over his cackling, "Get help! She's going to kill me!"

And just as I said that the door to my temporary safety shook, "I know you're in there SkyRocket!"

"Oh, shit," Nolan said more seriously, but his voice was still suspiciously breathy, "Is that her?"

"*Yes.* Now, will you focus!" I snapped as I adjusted my cell phone between my shoulder and cheek. Lifting both hands, I pushed the furniture against the door that wanted to burst at the seams. Again, not going to last, but it was at least something to block my crazy ex-friend, "I'm on the south side of town, about a fifteen-minute walk from that place you like to get milkshakes at-"

"How the fuck do-"

"Not the time!" I wanted to shout, but it came out more like a squeak of terror as the walls started to crumble. So I said the next bit in a rush of air, "Drop the assignment and hurry up!"

I didn't hear if he replied or not because the wall disappeared as if it was cargo getting shot out of an airlock, or maybe something flying out of an open plane. My phone slipped from my shoulder and onto the floor, the screen cracking and going dead.

"Finally," I heard Tamara say, and I rushed forward as I saw Tamara's red converse emerge from the destruction, stepping into my previously safe space. I propelled the furniture away to the back of the room and grabbed the doorknob of the door that was surprisingly still intact. I swung it open with all my strength, right into Tamara's face.

She screeched and stumbled back, holding her now bleeding nose between her fingers, "Mother-"

I didn't wait for her to finish her expletive because, at the moment, I only had two options:

1. Fight Tamara and/or escape her wrath. Or

2. Wait for Nolan.

Both equally sucky options.

The front of the shop was in utter disarray; it looked like a bomb had gone off. I leaped over the rubble, taking flight midjump, and focused as hard as I could at propelling myself forward. I had just passed the rails of the balcony when I heard Tamara ram her way out of the shop, her face angrier than I had ever seen and covered in a layer of blood.

Her boulder flying device crashed into the railing. Instead of taking it out and sailing forward, she jumped and tackled me in midair. My body spun downward, and I yelled as she wrapped her arms around my torso, her nails digging into my ribs through my shirt. She clawed and trashed, and I tried to dislodge her like a wild bull, but it only caused me to lose even more control, and I hit the first floor *hard*.

The air left my body, and Tamara scrambled until she was entirely on top of me, straddling my hips. Her eyes looked deranged, and the blood on the bottom half of her face could have been in a zombie movie; the red even caked in her teeth, *"Enough."*

Even though I was panicking, I managed a smirk, "Oh, yeah?"

Tamara's hair had fully come out of her ponytail in our tussle, and the curls framed her face, still damp from the rain. Holding me firmly in place with one hand, she brought the other up to wipe away some of the blood. Her wound hadn't stopped bleeding, and some of it dripped on my neck. And sure, I could have attacked her, could have done something at that moment to get her off, but a part of me was still hoping for the good in her, you know?

I didn't *want* to fight her, and I told her as much.

She growled and then viciously punched me. My head snapped to the side, and I blinked back in shock as Tamara demanded, "Just tell me, Skylar!"

"Why?" I spat back, and Tamara actually jumped.

"Why?" Tamara glowered, "Why!? Are you fucking serious right now?"

Was I? To be honest, I only said it to stall for time. To figure out how to get her off or give the backup more time to get to me. But then I realized that I wanted it to be serious.

Why?

Why was she a Super?

Why did she befriend me if she was only going to take me out in the end?

Just...*why?*

My face contorted, and in a fit of rage and betrayal, I shoved her off of me, harshly grabbing her shoulder and *pushing.* She flew sideways until she hit the bottom of the fountain, the water coating the floor splashing out around her as she skidded to a stop.

She groaned and pushed herself up at the same time as me, her clothes sticking to her frame.

We faced each other, and she violently flipped her hair out of her face, her words spiteful, "You think the world is so *black and white*."

"Don't put words in my mouth," I said as I started to rise into the air. My legs were beginning to throb, the lacerated cuts from the broken glass window to blame. All I could taste was iron. My face stung from the punch, but I continued anyway, "What about you? You think killing me will change anything?"

Tamara spits a wad of blood and saliva onto the floor, "It doesn't matter if it changes anything. I'll still be the 'evil' one either way!"

"You could use your powers for good!"

"Oh, fuck off! You think vigilantes can change the world!? What a load of *bullshit!*"

"It's not about changing the world! It's about keeping people safe from people like you!"

"Die!" Tamara screamed and snapped her arm up. The ground under me shot upward, and I barely dodged, the flooring flying off to land on the second floor. I turned back, and Tamara was already in front of me, snatching my ankle from the air and forcefully pulling me down. Once I was at eye level, she swung out with another well-aimed punch. I grabbed her arm before it connected and flipped her around, so I was closer to the fountain. She kicked out with her leg, and I ducked just in time.

There was no more room to talk; no more stalling.

Tamara was going to kill me.

I don't know how long we went on like that. It was a blur of jabs, punches, kicks, flying, skidding, flipping, and grapples. Tamara was telling the truth. She hadn't been trying, not really. I was wholly inexperienced, but I tried my best anyway. What choice did I have? I'm proud to say I got a few good hits in, proud that I almost escaped once or twice, but inevitably, it all came to a head at that damned fountain.

My vision was blurry, my breaths coming out in rasps. I was clutching my arm where at some point, Tamara had sliced the skin. I felt the blood leaking through my fingers and along my arm, dripping to the floor with a *plop, plop, plop*. My legs felt like they wanted to go numb, but the adrenaline refused to let them. My body was soaked to the bone from the rain.

I watched almost in slow motion as Tamara swung in for her attack, teeth bared like a rabid dog. I wanted to move, to try to dodge or block or do *something*, but I just couldn't focus. Tamara was only splotches of color in my eyes.

"Skylar!"

There was a flash, all blinding light, and I heard Tamara scream out in pain. Then, I felt something or someone grab onto my arm, and I stumbled sideways, the place that was held tingling with spasms and pain. Then, quickly, as if it was never there in the first place, the grip released, and all the strength in my legs left me all at once, and I collapsed to the floor.

I blinked back the blurriness, twitching in pain, to see Nolan standing in front of me, facing Tamara. His skin was shining, but there was something different about it. More sparks of color than a constant glow. I blinked a few times before I finally got out, "Whoa."

I watched as people swarmed Tamara, some I thought I recognized with my addled brain, but it was hard to tell. More importantly, at least at the time for past Skylar, I was focused on Nolan, "Holy sh-it is. . .that. . .?"

The flashes ceased on his skin, and he crouched down next to me, "What?"

"You were. . . spark-k-ling? Spark. . .s? Wh-ere you . . . al-ways. . .to do that?"

"Skylar, hey-"

And then everything caught up with me, and I passed out.

Though I would have loved to stay conscious out of spite because NOLAN EDWARDS can control *electricity!?!?*

When the hell did he learn that!?

☁ Chapter 16 ☁

I woke up with a raging headache.

And yes, it was an oh-my-god-this-is-the-worst-thing-to-happen-to-me-I'm-gonna-dieeeee kind of headache. And my whole body felt sore, too, like someone tenderized me before their meal. Or like I thoroughly got my ass whooped by my ex-friend in an abandoned mall.

You know, just your average dinner and a show.

After a long moment of just lying there, wondering if I really wanted to face the world yet, I moved to sit up. Something blocked me from going further, though, "Hey, now, don't do that just yet."

I groaned, my eyes still shut, and flopped back down on the infirmary bed. I couldn't see Oliver's smile, but for some reason, I knew it was on his face, "Glad you're awake. How are you feeling?"

"Like crap," I replied bluntly. I opened my eyes and looked at the ceiling in defeat, "Wow, deja vu."

Oliver snorted and then came into view, "Well, maybe you shouldn't get hurt then, huh?"

"Wow. Some doctor you are."

"Technically, I'm just a nurse," Oliver said with a shrug. He sat back in his office chair, and I turned my head so I could still look at him, "So, do you remember anything?"

"Other than utter betrayal? Yeah," I said irritably. Oliver just tilted his head and waited, and I let out a huff, "I remember fighting her and people showing up, but that's about it. Just blacked out after. . .after-I"

I sat up straight again, and Oliver grabbed my shoulders with a 'hey now!' but my mind was on other things, "And that Nolan was electrified! When the hell did he learn that!"

"Okay, I think I fixed your concussion," Oliver half-joked, and I was not in the mood for him to dodge my concerns! I stared into his soul as he slowly pushed me back down into the mattress, "As for Nolan, well, we think he could do that the whole time. He just never tried."

"But, but-I" I fumbled out, my hands flying up to gesticulate my point, "He glows. That's his thing! How did it turn into controlling electricity!?"

Oliver's eyebrows furrowed, "Light Bulbs use electricity, right? Maybe that's the link? I'm not sure, Skylar."

"It's just-why-it's-why'd he have to be *cool!?*" I said as I flopped down onto the bed, my hands covering my eyes, "How can I tease him now if I know he can zap me in retaliation? Or that he was secretly able to be a badass? Oh god, our whole dorm dynamic is about to change, and I *hate it!*"

Oliver leaned back and touched his chin in thought, "Hmm, well, if you mentioned how he electrocuted you during the rescue, he'll feel bad?"

"Wait, huh!?" I sputtered because when. . .oh. The bright flash and Tamara screaming. . .and the tingling pain. . ."You mean to tell me I'm in the infirmary again because of friendly fire?"

Oliver's mouth twitched despite how hard he tried to remain professional, "It would seem so. Though you were injured before he shocked you, so it wasn't all his fault. You would have been here regardless. But. . ."

I slowly brought my hands down and turned to face Oliver, very much like I wanted to stab him, "But?"

Oliver let out a long sigh, and it suspiciously sounded like regret, ". . .but you might have been out in time for exams if you didn't get electrocuted. . ."

I went to get up and forcibly discharge myself from the infirmary, so I could kill a particular roommate, but then another voice broke through my anger, "Don't worry about it, lie down!"

I paused with my bedsheets clenched in my fists, ready to fling them off my legs and make a run for it. On the other side of the room, leaning against the doorway was none other than you. You were wearing casual clothes, blue jeans, and a black long sleeve shirt. Arms crossed and hair tied back in a small ponytail, you oozed nonchalance.

You looked away, focusing your gaze on a handwashing PSA, "Don't worry about the exam. I think you did enough practical fighting to get a pass."

I stared at him suspiciously, "You just don't want to grade it."

You scowled, offended, "Do you want me to make you take a test before you leave in an hour because I can still do that."

I flopped back down and hoisted the blanket up to my chin, "Nope."

"Don't harass my patient," Oliver said seriously, but his smile gave him away, "Anyway, Skylar, same as last time. How many fingers am I holding up?"

"None," I said, not even looking at him.

"Okay!" Oliver said with a cheerful clap of his hands, "Memory checks out!"

My lips twitched, "So, am I healthy, Doc?"

"Yes, but I want to warn you that you might feel like you have jelly legs for the next few hours, along with the headache. I'll get you more painkillers for that, though," Oliver grunted as he got up and went to one of his medication cabinets.

As Oliver shifted bottles around to find what he was looking for, I turned back to face you, "Really though, no exams?"

"You owe me one," You waved off, "Besides, you did inadvertently capture the Superhero that was causing havoc around the island for months."

"Really..." I said, and I couldn't help but think that Tamara didn't seem like the type. And yes, I know we just had a smackdown and pretty much decimated a mall but at the same time...I got to know her over the few months I hung out with her. And maybe it was all a lie, maybe she pretended from the start like she said but...a part of me wanted it not to be an act. That she really did have fun with me when we played laser tag, went to the beach, and drank milkshakes..."What's going to happen to her?"

You gave me a look, considering, and Oliver paused from closing the cabinet door to listen.

"She's still a minor, so she won't get prison time. If I had to guess, she'll have to be on house arrest and mandatory community service. But she'll be under surveillance either way. Though. . ."

Oliver averted his gaze as you continued, "It's possible she won't be able to see her siblings until she finishes her sentence."

"Oh," I said for lack of anything else to say. Tamara only talked about her family once when we were looking out at the darkness of the ocean late one night. The moon was reflected off the water then, and I tried to pretend not to see the tears starting to form on the edges of her eyes. I still think about how she told me that she hasn't seen her parents in years, how she missed them. How she only had her two younger brothers and that she stayed with a family friend. How the only thing she had of her parents was her necklace. . .

And I knew deep in my heart that at least that moment with Tamara was genuine.

Because even Superheroes have a hard time faking sobs.

*****

Oliver wasn't kidding about the jelly legs. If the older students thought I was drunk the first time I left the infirmary, they really thought I was now. I stumbled my way back to the dorm to pack my stuff before I had to get back on the (UGH) boat in about forty minutes. It was so bad that you actually grabbed my arm and *helped me*. Maybe I looked like I was going to die? Because there was no way in hell that you would have helped me like that otherwise.

When I finally got to the dorm, it looked like that scene at the beginning of *Home Alone*. Jake and Chase were by the tv and were stuffing one of their duffle bags with movies. Layla was using her super-speed to run down the stairs instead of using the elevator, her luggage appearing suddenly one after another until she stopped with her hands on her hips, breathing hard. I could see Harley in the backyard, surrounded by animals and waving his arms around frantically. Others were exiting the elevator, squished together from lack of space.

"Oh, Skylar, you are back."

I screamed and jumped away from Ryuma. He smiled wide and was gripping the handle of his suitcase. With a hand on my heart, I said, "Yoshida, you scared the crap out of me."

"Ryuma."

"Huh?" I blinked back in surprise, wondering if my headache was making me hear things.

"You can call me Ryuma. Everyone else does now." Ryuma said, and part of me felt honored, but another part was angry that I wasn't there for the friend promotion and instead was added on as an afterthought. But either way, I was happy that Ryu wanted us to use his first name. Plus, now I don't have to write Yoshida anymore because that was Real. Weird.

"Okay, Ryuma. So, why is everyone running around with their heads cut off?"

Ryuma blinked, "But they have heads? I don't understand."

"Ah, no, I mean. . .it's an expression," I said dumbly. I just forget that Ryuma wasn't from the U.S. and still has a hard time with English. Though, to be fair, he has come a long way since the beginning of the school year. I am mega proud of him, "It means, uh, running around everywhere, I guess."

"Oh." Ryuma just shrugged, "We just got out of the final exam. Need to pack and go home."

"Ah, gotcha," I said even though I was a little confused why the last exam *just* ended. I looked at you from the corner of my eye, and the moment I saw the pleased look on your face, I understood.

You will always and forever be a sadist. Truly the incarnate of evil.

But I was kind of grateful that everyone was more focused on packing than *the incident.* Like I knew I was never going to live it down. The embarrassment of the impending teasing was bearing down on me, and I knew that I would have to enjoy the peace while I could. So, waving at Ryuma, I said I'd see him in a bit. I marched as fast as I could on my jelly legs to the open elevator and pushed the up button far more times than I really needed to.

You can't run from your fate forever, but you can surely give it your best shot. But in my rush, I didn't think about what I might face instead. And as I opened the door to my dorm, that miscalculation reared its ugly head; in the form of a startled Nolan Edwards.

Nolan froze mid-motion while putting a piece of clothing in his open suitcase. He turned away quickly, shoving the pair of shorts into his bag so hard it shook a little. His shoulders were tense, and maybe I should have read his body language a little better, but at the time, all I could get out was, "I'm going to kill you."

"Really?" Nolan said with a fair amount of bite, "Well, you can–"

"No, not really!" I yelled in exasperation, "But the thought did cross my mind!"

"Look," Nolan pushed out with noticeable effort but still managed to avert his eyes, "Whatever, be mad all you want about-"

"Why didn't you tell me you were secretly a badass!?" I continued, and Nolan blinked owlishly as he turned around, his expression still angry but now also scrunched up in confusion. Not one to be deterred, I went on, "Like, that information would have been nice to know when I needed my phone charged!"

"*What* the hell are you talking about!" Nolan exploded, "Why the fuck is that what you're mad about! *I electrocuted you!*"

"Oh, I'm mad about that too but-Just answer my question!"

"I don't know!"

"You don't know!? You're lying!"

"Oh, for the love of-" Nolan snarled. He marched over to me, and I felt the impending doom the moment he grabbed my shoulders, "I don't know, you fucking idiot! It just happened."

"It...just happened? Yeah, that's a legit excuse." I said, and the tables had turned. Now Nolan was the one that wanted to kill me, his glare intense, but I just stared at him down. A year of Nolan glares, coupled with knowledge about the snort-laugh, I was not afraid of Nolan.

Plus... we were friends after all.

Nolan shook my shoulder roughly, "It's not an excuse!"

"So then why, do you think?" I said mid-shake. Even I was starting to grow tired of teasing him, and the curious side of me was now winning the mental battle, "Things don't just happen like that..."

Nolan stopped in his attempt to mix the contents of my skull into soup. His mouth twitched as if his expression was at war with his brain, but finally, it settled into a fine-lined frown, "She was about to punch you. I just wanted to blind her so the others could..."

"Oh, I get it," I said smugly, "You had a 'power of friendship' moment. I'm honored it was because of me!"

"What, no!" Nolan recoiled instantly, backing away from me in a frantic backpedal. Nolan's lip curled, "Why would I help you? You disgust me."

"Aww, you disgust me too," I said, and Nolan just let out a very satisfying yell, "Shut up!"

"No. To think the Great Nolan Edwards would get to level up because he cares about someone. Truly a surprise!" The teasing was back full force, and I have to say, I was living my best life at that moment.

Maybe our dynamic didn't have to change that much, I thought, as Nolan hurled a wad of clothes at my head.

This was fine.

*****

Nolan got his revenge for the teasing when we went downstairs. I was right to assume that everyone wouldn't let me live *the incident* down. It was tease after tease, question after question, and by the time we all made it to the airport to leave, I was in embarrassment overload. I was glad that we would be on separate planes (normal ones, not private jets, which was a bit of a letdown).

Though some of the questions weren't teasing, just genuine worry, and it felt nice. It was nice to know that everyone cared. Even Adya gave me a harsh shove of affection as we went our separate ways. Over the school year, everyone had grown to be my second family...

And yes, I know that's sappy, but as I sat down in my seat, readying myself for the long flight back home, I couldn't deny that I was glad I decided to go to Freedom Bay Highschool. That I chose to seal my fate that day, one year ago. . .

And as I watched the island shrink below me, watched the water stretch out into the endless ocean, I knew, without doubt, that I didn't regret my decision.

Not one bit.

A few days later...

I really should have known that this would happen. Really, how could I not have seen this coming? You were too nice, and I should have seen the warning sign for what it was. But no, I bought your suspicious kindness hook, line, and sinker, like a fool.

And so, when I heard the doorbell ring, I got off the couch, totally unaware of what was to come. I grabbed the door handle and swung it open, "Alex! Mario kart or–"

"So, remember that favor you owe me?" You asked, and all I could do was stare, "Cause I want to cash in."

And...that was the moment I knew that my summer vacation was totally and utterly screwed.

TO BE CONTINUED...

About the Author:

Paridise Kau was born in northern California before moving to Montana her freshman year of Highschool. She always loved to write and wanted to get her stories out there for people to enjoy. She hopes that her readers will take something away from her work. . .even if it's just to give them a good chuckle! She also wants to thank you for buying her book! So, thank you!!

CPSIA information can be obtained
at www.ICGtesting.com
Printed in the USA
FSHW010701150921
84704FS